A Wizard's Curse Will Slowly Turn Her Into A Deadly Being

Morwen tried to release her grip, but couldn't, no matter how hard she struggled. Against her will, her hand's hold on the boy's neck grew tighter than ever as The Brand burned and stung and continued to slither down her arm.

She felt his neck bones crackle and snap as her hand closed all the way around his throat.

He wailed and pleaded through a torrent of tears. "Stop! Stop! Morwen, please stop! I'm sorry I attacked you! Help! Someone, HEEELP!! PLEEASE!!!"

"I can't let go! It won't stop!"

He went limp. A still, sickening silence fell upon the woods. The crickets stopped chirping, the frogs retreated under the surface of their shallow ponds, and the owls buried their beaks in their wings.

Morwen shut her eyes in fear of what she would see, as her hand slowly closed into a fist. A warm liquid flowed down her arm, and jagged objects poked out from between her fingers. The air filled with the faint aroma of copper. Morwen sniffed through petrified tears. A short popping noise and a soft hissing broke the silence as the liquid misted onto her face. Morwen opened her eyes, and her heart stopped.

She had ripped out his throat.

The Branding

Micaela Wendell

Bell Bridge Books

This is a work of fiction. Names, characters, places and incidents are either the products of the author's imagination or are used fictitiously. Any resemblance to actual persons (living or dead,) events or locations is entirely coincidental.

Bell Bridge Books
PO BOX 300921
Memphis, TN 38130
ISBN: 978-1-61194-009-1

Bell Bridge Books is an Imprint of BelleBooks, Inc.

Copyright © 2011 by Micaela Wendell

Printed and bound in the United States of America.

All rights reserved. No part of this book may be reproduced in any form or by any electronic or mechanical means, including information storage and retrieval systems, without permission in writing from the publisher, except by a reviewer, who may quote brief passages in a review.

We at BelleBooks enjoy hearing from readers.
Visit our websites – www.BelleBooks.com and
www.BellBridgeBooks.com.

10 9 8 7 6 5 4 3 2

Cover design: Debra Dixon
Interior design: Hank Smith
Photo credits:
Archers © Mike_Kiev | Dreamstime.com
Post work and manipulations to archers:
Alex White and Debra Dixon

:Lbt:01:

Acknowledgements

I'd like to give a very special thanks to Mrs. Julia Schuster. You helped me believe in myself and have the courage to achieve my dream. I'd also like to thank my parents and amazing friends for supporting me all through this crazy ride to publication. I love you all!

Chapter 1

As she bound her green hair behind her pointed ears, Morwen Aleacim listened for the gentle thump of her mother's and sister's footsteps downstairs. Not even a groan of a wooden floorboard echoed through the cottage, so she was safe. Morwen crept down the worn stairs and out the front door.

She rushed to a pile of firewood behind her family's two-story dwelling, an elegant yet sturdy structure. Patches of feathery moss grew thickly on its roof. Little birds pecked at the bugs that landed there.

Morwen's delicate hands lifted wooden logs from the pile, one by one, until she found what she wanted—the pathetic oak sword she had hidden at the bottom. The weapon's rough, disfigured blade showed her novice work at whittling, and its prickly handle often gave her splinters if she held it incorrectly.

Morwen set the sword aside while rebuilding the pile. When she'd finished, she picked up her sword, smiled at it for a moment, and ventured straight into the great forest—formally called the Silvia Forest—that surrounded her village of Aren.

Recently, there had been quite a few disappearances of young children in Aren, and their parents always told the same story: When their little one was playing at the edge of the woods under their watchful eye, they turned away for only a moment, and their son or daughter was gone.

A group of men banded together to search for the children. After they gathered weapons and armor and ventured into the woods, they never returned. Morwen's father, Arthil Aleacim, had been with them. Ever since his disappearance, Morwen had vowed to find him and the rest of the lost men.

However, the town elders greatly disapproved of anyone else risking a life. They wished to keep the elves of Aren *out* of the forest and the tragedy off of their minds.

Once she started wandering through the labyrinth of trees, Morwen's resolve withered. The tree shadows shifted into gangly monsters in the corner of her eye. The back of her neck prickled, and she began to wonder if she truly was alone in the forest. Morwen glanced over her shoulder, eyeing the trees and bushes behind her.

Her stomach tightened, and she turned back around. After breathing in to collect her courage, she wandered even farther into the woods. Morwen hoped that whatever snatched her father wouldn't snatch her, too.

After a while longer, as she continued her rather uneventful walk through the woods, Morwen relaxed a little and gained confidence. She smiled and twirled her fake sword, swatting low branches and drawing lines into moss patches nearby.

Morwen struck a tree and some shrubs. At one point, she hit a thistle bush. On impact, the sword made a hollow *clunk*, and the bush snarled. Startled, she carefully prodded it with her sword and stared into the tangled branches. She saw nothing, so she walked on.

The bush rustled behind her, and a low, prolonged growl rumbled from its branches. She turned around, and her heart leaped into her throat. A large hound lumbered from the brambles and raised its hackles.

Morwen stepped backward, readying her blade. The irritated animal, sporting three short, sharp horns on its head, growled more viciously than before. The creature's head lowered to charge. Morwen blinked, and the great beast was already soaring towards her. She swung her wooden sword towards the monster's maw of teeth. The hound latched onto the soft wood and tore it from Morwen's hand. She cried out when a large splinter slipped into her palm.

The wild dog stopped near her and waved the blade around with flips of its head. Its orange eyes watched her carefully. Morwen inched towards the creature, and it growled deep in its throat. When she came within arm's reach of the beast, it raised its head and snarled at her.

The sword fell from its mouth, and without thinking, Morwen dove after it, only to land right under the monster. Its head thrashed back and forth as its maw of teeth snapped at her. Morwen's head spun with indecision of what to do to save herself.

She closed her eyes and kicked upward as hard as she could. She hit nothing. The monster's massive jaws flew toward her throat. She screamed and kicked again. The hound jerked, howled weakly . . . and collapsed. Its immense weight nearly crushed her small body.

Morwen struggled to breathe, but the hound kept her chest from rising at all. She squirmed and attempted to push the monster off her. A strong hand appeared and sank into the animal's thick fur. That hand pulled on the hide, and the dog carcass quickly rolled off her.

"Are you all right, young lady?"

Gasping for air, Morwen looked up and saw a tall human man, fatherly and older. The silver streaks in his black hair, beard and moustache showed his age, but his eyes held that little spark of youth and life inherent in all adventurers. He gazed down at Morwen as if her pointed ears and green hair made *her* the oddity.

Armando. No one knew his surname. He was the only human living in Aren, but the elven elders did not force the retired adventurer out of town. The elders considered him a curiosity, a living example showing the elves how real humans lived and behaved. They agreed to let him stay as long as he didn't cause trouble. They didn't worry about him much, for Armando, somewhat of a recluse, had no contact with the elves in the past ten years.

He was not a friend to the elves, nor were the elves friends with *him*. In general, the elders considered humans a bad influence. Supposedly, humans' laxness in following the traditions of their ancestors was a disgrace. Humans were fickle, as the elven children were told. Men were always changing their way of life and altering how things worked.

They "disrespected the work of their forefathers," as the elders had taught, but Morwen knew in her heart that humans simply wanted to *build* upon their predecessors' ideas, not defile them.

Armando held out a hand.

Morwen finally caught her breath. "Thank you." She grabbed his hand, and he hoisted her to her feet. His physical strength matched that of a man ten years his junior.

But then he stumbled, favoring a leg. "Cursed old knee," he said. He steadied himself, then looked down at her grimly. "I cannot believe you went into the woods deliberately looking for trouble."

"But I . . . " she said, her voice trailing off.

"But what?"

"Nothing." Morwen said, looking to the dead creature. Its sides were soaked in blood. "Is that thing dead?"

"Yes, thankfully," Armando said, rubbing his long sword's bloody blade on his trousers. "Young lady, why in heavens were you out here? I'm quite familiar with the woods, you know, and I'm *positive* it's not a place for a little elf like you."

"Little? Excuse me, Mr. Armando, but I am fifteen elf years old! *And* I am just about five feet tall."

"Ah, yes, the we-age-four-years-slower-than-you pride. I have heard of that too many times to count."

"We age *three* years slower than you."

"Close enough. For all those years you've been alive, I thought you'd have much more wisdom than this. But you know what they say about assuming things . . . "

"The elders don't let young elves do anything unless the 'Old Ways' allow it."

"I guess they are just keeping you from maturing too quickly. Their reasons are sound. I have seen now how reckless young elves like you can be."

Morwen sighed. She picked up her chewed wooden sword and said, a little annoyed, "Well, thank you again for rescuing me, but I must get home now. I'll return to practice my sword play another time." She started to walk away. "I intend to become a warrior so I can find Father and the others. I must push myself down that path, even if I have to do it alone."

Armando thought for a second and asked, "Do you honestly wish to become a fighter?"

Morwen stopped. "Yes, but I thought you disapproved of my fighting."

"I disapprove of your recklessness, not your courage and heart. Not *every* proper young elf has the nerve to walk into the woods alone. Especially female elves, considering the laws and everything."

"Are you trying to give me a compliment?"

"You *are* brave, but you need more than that to survive on the path you've chosen. Listen, these woods are filled with things a million times worse than that hound you just faced. Wizards can snatch you away if your guard is down. Trolls and were-boars can crush your bones into oblivion. Snakes and demons can strangle you from behind. If you want to become a fighter—"

"A warrior," Morwen corrected him.

"It's the same idea. Regardless, you still need proper training."

"Training? I've been working hard for eight months, now! I even made my own weapon. I doubt I need further instruction."

Armando lifted his sword and swung it at Morwen. She grabbed her own weapon from the ground and tried to block him. Armando's superior iron blade sliced through the worn wood, and the feeble little sword broke in two. Morwen's hand remained on the severed hilt.

"What weapon? All I see is a broken child's toy," Armando said with a smile.

Morwen frowned. He had destroyed her beloved blade. "If you think I need training so badly, then why don't *you* train me?"

"That was my thought in the first place. I just wanted to see if you were open to the idea."

"I am, but the emperor won't allow women to learn to fight."

"The emperor can go chew my boot. I'd gladly to train you, if you're willing to take on the challenge."

Morwen's brow furrowed. "We have one problem, though . . . I can't be seen swinging a sword around in plain sight, let alone with a human."

"You'll meet me here. We'll practice each morning, right after dawn, before everyone wakes up."

"Alright, but how can I trust you, Mr. Armando?"

He counted on his fingers. "Firstly, I killed the wild dog before it killed *you*. Secondly, I didn't decide to slice you in half after I broke your weapon. And lastly, I blatantly spoke against the emperor and trusted that *you* wouldn't turn me in. Do you think that's enough?"

Morwen nodded.

"Then I'll see you tomorrow morning."

Armando and Morwen shook hands, and the elf said slowly, "Handshakes are just handshakes, Mr. Armando. I'll still be wary."

"That's a good first step. *Never* let your guard down."

Morwen tossed the splintered remnants of her sword aside and ran home. She thought about all the young elven girls in town who followed tradition and married young elven boys.

They then produced large families and followed the elders' every decree. They were merely sheep penned in Aren under the elders' rule. Morwen herself wished to be something more than a mate and housekeeper. Marrying around sixteen—in elf years—made her uneasy.

Deep in her heart, Morwen knew she could never alter her culture's rigid traditions. Back in her head, she kept a plan to escape from Aren and become a fierce, famous warrior . . . Perhaps other elven girls would follow her example. Until then, Morwen dreamed of the day she would pack up her belongings and run to her destiny.

She knew Armando could help her. She knew he could give her the tools and skills to make her dreams become reality. She knew something big would happen to her soon—she could just feel it—and she knew Armando was the only person who could help her prepare for it.

Chapter 2

Three years passed. Morwen's skills had improved tremendously throughout training, but her fighting talent had yet to match Armando's years of experience.

Their swords crashed together with the intent to kill. They parted and met again, conjuring a little fountain of sparks. Morwen jabbed her blade at Armando's heart. He slid out of the way before it hit him. He limped a bit on his bad leg, but he still managed to sidestep behind her.

He raised his blunt claymore above her head of pine-green hair. Morwen twisted her fingers along her sword's hilt, and her blade flew behind her in an upward arc. The steel met the chain mail in Armando's armpit with a faint *clunk*. Armando's weapon fell to the trampled grass, and he raised his hands—scarred and worn—over his head.

"Excellent, Morwen. Truly remarkable." He grinned at his pupil. Morwen smiled back, her hazel eyes widening in excitement and pride.

Now sixteen in elf years, Morwen had become unbelievably talented—and beautiful. She attracted the envy of many in Aren with her flowing hair and her smooth skin. Instead of flaunting her looks like any proper elven girl would, Morwen tried to downplay them as much as she could.

She started every day with simply brushing her hair and donning her so-called "boy clothes." Many women in Aren complained to the elders that Morwen displayed no desire to marry at the moment, and they insisted that she be coerced to think otherwise.

The town wanted pretty baby elves, not a rebel. Morwen had never confessed that she craved danger, travel, and quests, but the elders were getting suspicious.

Armando had also changed over the past three years. Instead of sporting a salt-and-pepper head of hair and beard, he now had a wispy, white tonsure and fluffy facial hair. He'd admitted to her that he was now fifty-nine in human years, and he knew and accepted that he was not as nimble as he was decades ago.

His bad leg had worsened, and scars and wrinkles covered his hands. His great wisdom showed that he had lived his life well, and that whenever his time came, he would go with no regrets.

Armando pushed her blade away from his armpit and chuckled. "Wonderful job! Now, I think we can move on to more advanced techniques. They will, however, be quite tricky. Do you think you're ready?"

"I'm up to any challenge!"

"That's the spirit! Now go stand by my hut. You'll be out of range there."

Morwen did as he instructed.

"Now, watch me closely."

Armando picked up his silver claymore from the dew-dotted grass. He held it in front of his face and closed his eyes in concentration. Morwen held her breath in quiet anticipation. She watched him jab his sword upward. Armando swung his blade down with all his might and drove its tip into the ground.

Jets of fire and yellow sparks erupted from the penetrated ground. Morwen shielded her eyes as the magical bursts stretched away from Armando and flailed in all directions, creating a deadly barrier around him. The sheer power of the magic conjured a small whirlwind that twirled Morwen's hair into tangles and knots.

Armando drew his sword from the dirt, and the flames and sparks retreated into the earth like cockroaches caught in sunlight.

Morwen's skin prickled with excitement. "That was fantastic!"

Suddenly, Armando dropped to his knees and leaned forward in exhaustion. He wiped the sweat from his brow with his ragged shirt sleeve and wheezed. Morwen hurried over to him and kneeled down at his side. Deeply worried, she took his heavy sword from his hands. Armando coughed and said, "Do you see? This is . . . tricky. It wears you out."

"But that's only a small setback, right?"

"No. This technique puts you at risk, because if it doesn't harm or kill your enemy when you first use it, it will leave you very weak. The enemy will have a clear shot at you that you don't want him to have."

Morwen slid her arm around his back and helped him hobble to a nearby tree stump to rest. After sitting down, Armando thanked her and said, "Now you try it, Morwen. Just copy my movements and focus all your energy to the tip of your blade."

"Yes, sir."

Morwen picked up her short sword and stood in the center of that clearing behind Armando's hut. She held her sword in front of her face and closed her eyes. She concentrated, and a strange tingling sensation surfaced on the tips of her fingers. She opened her eyes and swung the sword downwards, driving it into the soft earth below.

Morwen awaited a massive wave of energy like Armando's, but only a tiny spark squeezed from the ground and drifted lazily around her head. It landed on the grass and ignited a few dry blades. Armando chuckled. Morwen stomped out the fire as quickly as she could.

Armando put his hands on his knees and pushed himself to his feet. He grinned at Morwen in reassurance. "Ah Morwen, you were so close. Try again."

She nodded, smiling.

Morwen held the sword up to her face yet again and focused, but her concentration broke when a familiar, birdlike cry echoed through the forest. That concerned song could only come from one person—her mother.

"I'm sorry, but I need to leave," Morwen said. "I think we've been training for too long today . . . ."

"I understand. Now go. Just tell your mother that you went to the stream nearby to fish or some story like that. I'll see you tomorrow."

Morwen handed her sword to Armando and turned on the spot. Bursting into a run, she hurried through the misty morning sunlight towards her house. She darted past the simple cottages and tiny shops of the town and politely greeted her neighbors with a quick wave and a smile.

Morwen trotted to a halt at her house's front steps and dusted herself off. She opened the front door. Inside, her mother leaned over a metal tub on the counter and cleaned the morning's used pots and pans. The bright sunbeams swimming through the window exaggerated her mother's soft features and the long brown hair that swept behind her pointed ears.

Morwen's six-elf-year-old sister Brynn sat at the oak table gobbling up her hearty breakfast of bacon, eggs, and goat milk. She caught her black locks in her fork and stuffed them into her mouth on accident.

As Morwen walked through the door, Brynn's eyes widened and she squealed through a mouth stuffed with hair and eggs, "Wook! Mowen's heewe."

Without turning from her work, Morwen's mother, Tena Aleacim, asked in her high voice, "Where were you, Morwen? I was wondering where you went."

Morwen grinned. "Oh, I just went to the stream to relax, don't worry." Morwen strode across the wooden floor and pulled up a creaky chair next to her sister.

Mother said, "You know I don't like it when you leave the house without telling me, especially if you're dressed like you are. Everyone notices. None of us understand why you prefer to dress like a boy."

"I apologize." She snatched a thick strip of bacon from her sister's plate.

Brynn swallowed quickly and whined, "Morwen stole my food!"

"How about I make you your *own* breakfast so you won't have to feed off your sister's?"

"Yes, please."

Mother began cooking at the black iron stove, her smile quiet, content to be a traditional elven woman. Every once in a while she would sadly glance out the window to the tree where she had last kissed her now missing husband. When the meal was ready, she served it on a clay plate without a word.

Morwen finished her breakfast minutes later, and she pushed her plate and fork away. Mother picked them up and placed them near the tub to clean later, and then she grabbed her satchel of gold coins and her shopping basket.

She turned to Morwen as she walked toward the front door. "I am going to market today. How about you two come with me this time. It is such a fine day."

"Alright," the sisters said in unison.

"But Morwen, please dress like a proper young lady. Do you want everyone in town scolding and teasing you again?"

"I have gotten used to it."

Mother sighed. "You know what happened to that Aleck boy when he pushed his luck with the elders. He was banished into the forest. The forest! Please, Morwen, at *least* put on a skirt for me."

"If you insist," Morwen grumbled, stomping up the stairs. She entered her bedroom and pulled a long skirt out of her drawers. She wrapped it around her hips and fastened it tightly over her leather pants. Morwen came down the stairs again. Brynn hopped down from her chair in her little white chemise and slippers and ran to her mother's side.

Mother opened the heavy front door and let her two daughters run outside. She closed it behind her.

Brynn danced around the dirt road and twirled so that her skirt would rise into a spinning flower of cloth. Morwen walked with silent dignity, as befitted a warrior in training. She watched the morning sun stroke the mossy roofs of nearby houses.

Morwen admitted that her stuffy little town *was* quite pretty. Intricate, twisting carvings fell like vines over each building's elegant log woodwork. Every elven house looked the same as the next, and each shop was a small replica of a house. That uniformity was the standard in elven society, which explained why Armando's human house, with its plain and stony simplicity, made the people of Aren a little nervous.

Morwen and her family passed Mrs. Ruwen's house. Ruwen sat upon her front steps, stitching stars onto a little blanket draped over her large, round belly. Her straight, copper-red hair fell to her waist, giving her a soft and fair appearance. She looked up from her work and smiled.

"Well hello, Tena, Morwen, Brynn."

"When do you think he will arrive?" Mother asked, smiling at Ruwen's belly.

Ruwen put a slim hand on her stomach. "I am sure he will come soon. He kicks me unceasingly, now. But I must ask—how are you faring?"

Mother's smile faded. Ruwen set her work aside and smiled politely, her brow furrowing. "It has been three years, Tena. Three. I know you love him, but—"

"But what? That I should give up on him as quickly as the elders did?" Her eyes filled with tears.

Morwen cringed, and Brynn fell silent.

"No, but I am just saying that you should spare yourself the pain and let go of him now."

"I have already endured three years of pain. Giving up after only three years is for fools, just like the eld—" She caught herself before she could finish. Ruwen, shocked, said nothing.

Mother collected herself and said, "It was pleasant speaking to you, Ruwen, and I hope you and Filliper are well until we meet again." She turned on the spot and walked away quickly.

The girls and their mother continued down the road in silence. Morwen smiled to herself with a newfound respect for her mother. They turned the corner and heard the hum of the small marketplace nearby. The striking aroma of fresh fish and meat, and the sweet scent of bread filled the air. They turned another corner and found the first set of booths dotting the road. Only twenty-four stalls had been set up that day, and each shopkeeper politely advertised his or her wares to passers-by. A strange prickling sensation tickled the back of Morwen's neck, and she looked to her left.

A group of five teenage boys had gathered at the side of the road. Ailben, Caelian, Daehel, Nym, and Syltas all watched her with smiles on their faces. The elders supposedly had proclaimed these young elves as "perfect gentlemen," but in actuality these boys harassed Morwen to no end. Ailben was a quiet elven boy sporting long, white-blonde hair, and Caelian stood next to him and winked at Morwen with his dark eyes. Daehel and Nym were identical twins, and each of them wore their long, black hair in thin braids that swished in the breeze.

Syltas, the "leader" of the group, puffed out his chest and smiled at Morwen. He had a sick mind, and his actions towards Morwen could hardly qualify as behavior befitting a gentleman. His long, golden blonde hair and subtle arrogance made any girl swoon in his presence, but Morwen hardly took notice of him.

Morwen walked closer to her mother's side and watched them from the corner of her eye. Mother, however, went on shopping without noticing her daughter's change of behavior.

"It seems like Morwen's scared of you, Syl!" Nym said loudly.

Morwen stopped and turned around. Her mother continued through the market, oblivious. "I'm not scared. I just *don't like you*—any of you," she said, her eyes flickering to Syltas.

"Are you still upset about me kissing you last week?" Syltas said.

Morwen wiped her lips with her hand in remembrance. "Why wouldn't I be?"

"Ah, calm down. You fail to appreciate how attractive you really are. It's the truth. I can show you how pretty you are *tonight*, if you'd like. Just meet me at the creek tonight and we can take a tumble in the reeds together."

"How dense do you think I am?" Morwen asked, slapping him across the cheek.

Syltas, shocked, touched his throbbing side of his face. The teenage comrades behind him *oohed* muttered to each other. His nostrils flared. "How *dare* you slap me!"

"It's punishment appropriate for a brute like you."

Syltas balled his fists, but his friends grabbed him and held him back. "Brute? Look at yourself—you speak against the elders, you dress like a man, and you strike others on a whim. I'm starting to believe the elders . . . you probably *are* a demon! Morwen, deeply hurt from his comment, turned and hurried after her mother, who had just turned the corner.

Morwen rushed around the curve in the road and stopped. Mother was nowhere in sight. Morwen's stomach tightened as she looked up and down side lanes. Morwen was now alone on the very street where all the elders took residence. She took a deep breath and walked down the road. She stood tall with her shoulders back and did her best to appear confident. At any second, the cranky old elves could fly out of their homes and—

"Morwen Aleacim!"

"Yes, *Lady Cassade?*"

"You are wearing a man's shirt again! And trousers under your skirt!"

"I—"

"I don't know why I haven't banished you for your disrespectful defiance. I think the demons from Sanguine must have possessed you again. Thorian! Thorian, get the feathers!"

Lady Cassade, who was exactly a hundred elven years of age, was one of the sterner enforcers of the "Old Ways." Whenever Morwen tried to discuss altering elven rules at all, Lady Cassade would give her a wrinkly scowl and hurry to expel the "demon" inside of her.

Lady Cassade and her husband, ninety-elf-years-old Thorian, came out of the cottage clutching hawk feathers and a bowl of burning incense. The tall, thin elders danced around in their flowing, cream-colored robes and waved the stifling scent into Morwen's face. Lady Cassade and Thorian hummed and chanted for all of Aren to hear. Elf faces peeked out windows to watch the spectacle. Morwen waited for the old couple to finish. She felt her face and welling tears grow hot.

The ritual quickly ended, and Lady Cassade asked, "Dear Morwen, do you wish to become a *proper* young lady, now?"

Morwen clenched her fists and held her head high. "Not really, but good day to you." She walked off, trying not to reveal her ever-rising anger and humiliation.

Thorian said from behind, "Have you ever thought that she might *not* have a demon in her? She just may be one *herself.*"

Morwen sniffed and sprinted off to find her mother.

"Morwen, dear, are you alright?" Mother asked when her daughter approached.

Morwen knew the heat in her cheeks had turned them bright red. Her eyes, glossy with tears, ruined her chances of denying she was upset at all. "I'd like to go home, please," Morwen said quickly. "Lady Cassade went on one of her rampages. She tried to smoke a demon out of me again."

"I told you that you shouldn't wear those clothes outside."

Morwen gave up on arguing about it right then and there. Mother shifted her attention when Brynn tugged on her skirt.

The little girl's face scrunched into an anxious grimace. "Mother! Please, *please* can you play with me? Please?"

"I'm sorry, but I still have a lot to do. Maybe Morwen can play."

Brynn's huge blue eyes watched her sister.

Morwen sighed. "Fine. Where do you want to go, then?"

"Over there!" she said, pointing to the edge of the Silvia Forest.

Mother turned pale. "Do *not* go near there."

"Of course we won't," Morwen said, smiling a little. She led her Brynn a ways down the road and made a sharp turn to the edge of the forest. Oh, how Morwen loved testing her luck.

"We were told not to play here," Brynn said.

Morwen sat down and weaved a few blades of grass through her fingers. "There's nothing bad about the woods. As long as we don't travel too deeply into it, we'll be fine."

Brynn waddled nervously to the edge of the Silvia Forest and stared into the tapestry of trees and bushes. She asked, "Are you sure? A—Are there any monsters in there?"

Morwen thought for a moment. "Well, there is that thing that keeps taking the children here."

Brynn sat next to her sister, her eyes wide with curiosity. "What is it? Is it a monster?"

"Nobody knows what it is, really, but I think it's that evil wizard from the fables."

"*Tobias?*"

"Yes, him. No one here will believe me, though. Wait, why do you want to hear such a scary story, anyways?"

"Mother won't tell it to me, but I know you will."

"Maybe she won't tell you because it will give you nightmares."

"I won't be scared with *you* here, Morwen. You're brave. You can stand up to the elders and all the boys in town."

Morwen smiled and said, "But don't you try copying my actions, understand? Not yet, at least. I don't know how you can handle what I go through each day."

A nearby bush shook. Morwen rested her chin in her hand and watched a little white rabbit stumble into view.

"Is—Is that an *evil* rabbit, Morwen?"

"You've been listening to the elders too much. Rabbits are harmless."

The shy, furry animal stared at the sisters. Its ears twitched, and it bounced back into the woods. Brynn and turned to her sister.

"Can you tell me the story, now, Morwen?"

"Of course," she said, making herself comfortable on the ground. "Well, about a century ago, Tobias worked for the Good King, Dragomir, in the Luminescent, his castle. At that time, Tobias's name was Fidel, and he was Dragomir's most trusted advisor. As time went on, Fidel answered dark magic's alluring call and embraced it. He soon made a deal with Belial, the King of Sanguine, to become a Dark Wizard."

Morwen looked at her sister. "Let's stop. You're getting really scared."

"N—No, I'm n—not scared!"

"Then why are you stuttering?"

"I—I'll be brave, just like you."

Morwen smiled and continued the tale. "Eventually, King Dragomir discovered Fidel's secret, and he expelled him from the castle. Out of shame and a wish to sever ties with his lighter side, Fidel changed his name to Tobias and replaced his white garments with black wizard robes.

Tobias traveled thousands of miles across the ocean from his home country, Hyacinth, to arrive here on Farrfala. The legend also says that the entrance to Sanguine lies in the southern part of Farrfala."

Brynn's breathing grew shallow, and she scooted even closer to Morwen.

"Tobias stayed holed up in Sanguine for two hundred years and allowed his demon powers to devour his soul, but he still retained his youthful looks. But every day since his full immersion in dark magic, he's been preparing to kill Dragomir with a 'perfect evil' that is supposedly the king's only weakness. Tobias wants revenge, and that's why he kidnaps little children. He wants to experiment on them in his underground workshop and turn them into nasty, destructive creatures of death."

"Why would Tobias take Father and the other men?"

"Well . . . nobody knows if it was Tobias who took them. Don't worry, though; nobody can defeat Father."

Brynn, excited, stood up and cried, "He'll free all of them and march home. Then we'll have a great celebration to welcome them back to Aren!"

"Some day. But back to the story, we know that Tobias hasn't succeeded in creating his prized monster, yet," Morwen said. "That's why he's looking to take away a special child from Aren."

Brynn's lower lip quivered. "Th—That's not true! Tobias isn't going to take any more children. Mother told me so."

"Believe what you want, but I have the feeling he might be watching us . . . right now."

Brynn glanced around. "Please don't talk about Tobias anymore. Can we play a game?"

"Like what?"

"Let's play tag, and you're it."

Brynn poked Morwen in the arm and ran away, giggling. Morwen let her sister get a head start, and she ran after her once she was far enough away. She caught up to her easily, and she was able to trap Brynn between two houses.

She patted Brynn on the head. "You're it!" She turned on the spot and sprinted into the forest. Brynn followed Morwen to the edge and stopped. Looking over her shoulder, Morwen called, "There's nothing dangerous here! Don't be scared!"

She slowed to a halt, watching Brynn take a few nervous steps into the woods. Her little hands clutched her skirt, and her wide eyes darted left and right.

"See? It's not bad at all!"

Brynn let go of her skirt and began running towards Morwen. Morwen ran slowly as to not lose her sister. The cool forest hair played with her hair, and the fresh smell of pine trees and moss freed her senses from the stuffy village experience. Her paces grew longer . . . faster . . . until she was in a full-on run. Weaving through the trees and swinging from low branches, Morwen lost herself in the moment.

Brynn screamed behind her.

Morwen stopped and turned around, retracing her steps. "Brynn? Brynn, are you alright?" Her heart raced as she pushed through thick bushes and saplings. Soon, she came upon Brynn, who was sobbing and hugging a scraped knee.

"What happened?"

"I tripped—I tripped on a l-log in the path."

Morwen glanced at the trail behind Brynn. There were no logs blocking the path.

She helped her little sister to her feet. "Come now, you probably just tripped over your own feet . . . "

Brynn's eyes widened in terror. "MORWEN, WATCH OUT!"

Morwen spun around, ready to fight. No one was there. She squinted into the distance. Still, she saw nothing. A little relieved, yet a little uneasy, Morwen sighed.

"Brynn, what on *earth* did you see behind me?" No response.

"Brynn?" She turned around, and Brynn was gone. "Oh no."

Her heart flying up into her throat, Morwen ran through the woods screaming her sister's name. She kept telling herself that Brynn might have wandered off, but her gut told her that something was seriously wrong.

The running fatigued her quickly, and she slowed to a walk as she passed a mud puddle. Large divots and a tan lump decorated the slop. Morwen turned away as if it was nothing, then looked back. That tan lump looked just like a little shoe. Crouching down near the muck, she pinched the object and picked it up. It was a small slipper, and when she inspected it more closely, she found a messily scrawled "Brynn" on the underside of the shoe's sole.

Morwen looked up. The holes were not random depressions at all—they were footprints. Morwen's eyes widened, and she jumped to her feet. With her sister's shoe in hand, Morwen, almost in tears, followed the tracks. She clenched the shoe in her palm. She had pushed her luck too far this time.

The muddy trail soon came to an end, and Morwen threw down the slipper in frustration. She paced frantically. *What do I do! What do I do!* A faint hissing noise and the sound of bubbling water caught her attention.

As hope slowly returned to her, Morwen listened carefully. *This way*, she said to herself. The odd noise led her eastward. The din grew louder as she approached its source.

Morwen followed the racket to a small clearing where a massive boulder stood, its center hollowed out into a tunnel that led into the ground. The inner walls of the tunnel flickered with an ominous red-orange light. Her head spinning from the deafening clamor, Morwen pressed her hands over her ears and inched towards the tunnel, knowing in her heart that whatever—or whoever—took Brynn had gone down there with her.

Morwen stepped through the doorway and onto the stairs chiseled into the floor. The racket died in an instant, and the only sound that reached her ears was the quaking drum-dance of her panicked, frantic heart.

Chapter 3

Slowly and warily, Morwen tiptoed down the steps. Armando had taught her that underground creatures were the most deadly of all, so she kept her guard up.

Most of the monsters from Sanguine had gained enhanced hearing and smell in exchange for their sight. Morwen strained her ears for a sound from Brynn. The eerie glow and the dust-laced air burned her eyes, but she forced herself to keep them open so she wouldn't trip on the jagged, uneven stairs.

After Morwen had descended for a while, she paused when a painfully icy, invisible hand suddenly grabbed her ankle. She gasped as goose-bumps raced up and down her spine.

The hand slinked up her body, stopping at her chest bone. The hand slowly sank into her rib cage and grabbed her heart. Its frosty palm shocked the hot, beating muscle. She doubled over, wincing from the numbingly cold pain.

The hand constricted her heart, and she dropped to her knees, hugging her ribs. Morwen tried to scream, but when she opened her mouth, nothing came out. **She pushed as hard as she could to make even the slightest sound, but all she managed was a crackling gag, and a large spurt of blood burst from her mouth.** She wiped the blood from her lips and reached outward for a savior.

She coughed weakly. Morwen hung her head in defeat and spat to get rid of the blood's bitter, metallic taste. The saliva that dribbled from her mouth landed on an invisible *something* in front of her rather than the floor. The spit-stained thing rose and fell, as if it were breathing. Morwen feebly felt around for its source. She found a long, bumpy, and soggy object leading to her heart.

Morwen used both of her hands to latch onto the invisible creature in front of her. She tried her hardest to pull the monster's hand from her chest, but it only gripped her heart harder. Her breastbone bowed dangerously with her tugging.

The fiend squeezed even more on her beating heart, and a throbbing numbness branched from her chest down to her left arm. A wave of dizziness struck Morwen, and her breathing grew shallow. A quick pitter-pattering vibrated in her chest.

Morwen's heart desperately attempted to pump blood and beat faster. Seconds later, it slowed to only a few beats every five seconds . . . ten seconds . . . twelve seconds. Suddenly, as if it had been shocked by lightning, it leaped inside her chest again and pumped as rapidly as it could without bursting. Morwen gasped for air like a beached fish.

Morwen reached down her shirt and located the tiny, hidden dagger that hung on a black cord around her neck—she kept it to fight off Syltas and his group if they ever got out of hand.

Morwen, struggling with her chest pain and loss of air, drew the dagger from its leather sheath and drove it into the creature. Bright green blood spurted from the point of impact with a faint misting noise. Thicker blood flowed from the creature in a river that created a large puddle below.

The creature emitted an ear-shattering screech that echoed through the tunnel. Emerging from a magical mist, the abomination appeared at last. The monster—that glob of bloody, moldy, gray flesh—swayed slowly from side to side, its nasty skin groaning with each movement.

Open sores and scabs striped its bloated right arm and leg, and its left arm and leg were bare, cracked bone with a bits and pieces of flesh still stuck to them. This thing was a living, walking, half-eaten carcass.

The head of the beast terrified Morwen the most. Her stomach churned uneasily at the sight of it. Fungus-crowned brains spilled from its cracked skull, and its milky white, pupil-less eyes and sagging, toothless jaw froze Morwen stiff in shock.

The creature made a long, drawn-out croak, and squeezed Morwen's heart tighter. The creature breathed in with a loud wheeze, and Morwen's heart relaxed from its fast pumping. Glowing green veins appeared on the monster's arm where it connected with Morwen's heart.

The color slithered up the veins until it reached the creature's own heart. Its body swelled, growing in size. Its grip grew tighter than ever, making Morwen's heart race once again. She now understood—this creature lived off of another's life force.

Shocked by her realization, Morwen's heart pumped so fast inside her that she thought it would jump right out of her chest. Suddenly, it relaxed and pumped much slower than it had before.

The beats of her heart weren't the little thumps in her chest anymore. They were the loud, deafening throbs of noise that filled her ears like water and knocked against her head. Moments felt like years in her daze. The world blurred, and the walls bulged and warped around her. *Is this how it feels to die?* She was so tired, so sleepy . . . An image of a small, black-haired girl appeared in her head.

No, she could not let herself die. She *had* to save Brynn.

Morwen, despite her exhaustion, used the last of her strength to plunge the dagger into the creature's heart. The blade easily sank into the loose, rotting flesh.

Neon-green blood spewed from the wound in torrents. The creature released Morwen's heart, and it tore its hand from her chest. Her heart pumped madly, trying to bring itself back to its normal rhythm.

The monster let out a long, deep croaking sound, and its legs gave away. It fell backwards to the ground. Morwen tried to pull her hand away from the implanted dagger, but she slipped on the blood and fell onto of the corpse.

As she caught her breath, the creature's body began sliding down the stairs. They gained speed quickly, so Morwen had no chance to roll off of it. They flew down the endless flights of stairs at breakneck speed. A neon green stripe marked the path behind them.

Morwen held her eyes wide in terror, while trying to keep her head from smacking the wall as she flew down the bumpy stairs. She passed a jagged rock sticking out from the wall, and it caught the right shoulder of her shirt, tearing off the sleeve. At last, the dead body slowed to a halt and went limp.

The frightened elf rolled off and sprang to her feet, ready to pounce on it again for an attack. The monster's body convulsed, and its flesh bubbled as if boiling. The creature melted into a puddle of metallic, neon green sludge in one long, drawn-out hiss.

Morwen fell to her knees and dropped her dagger onto the floor. She bent over and sprawled onto the hard steps. She was still trying to take in what had just happened: she had almost, *almost* died. How fragile she was.

How vulnerable she was to the powers of evil. Morwen sighed heavily, blinking back tears, and shook her head to get rid of the haunting thoughts. She *had* to be strong. She *had* to rescue Brynn.

Chapter 4

Relieved that the creature was dead and that her pain had faded away, Morwen stood and continued down the never-ending staircase. The monotonous scenery lulled her into a bored daze, but a dull cackle bounced through the tunnel and snapped her into her senses. She froze, straining her ears to hear if someone—or *something*—had found her.

A creepily soothing voice echoed from nearby. "Ahh, little Brynn...."

Fueled by a second wave of determination, Morwen crept quickly down the steps. She turned another corner of the staircase and found a landing with a looming doorway framed by red stone. The staircase descended on past it.

Staying as quiet as possible, almost forgetting to breathe, Morwen hugged the wall and inched towards the doorway. Once she was next to it, she carefully peered into the room behind it, careful to keep herself hidden.

The somewhat large, underground room was a muddy tan, and magical symbols and tiny notes in indigo ink splashed the walls. A sturdy wooden workbench stood on the room's far left. Bizarre, tube-like fungi grew out of it and sagged from the weight of their spores.

Shrunken heads hung above the workbench in abundance, while dozens of black candles burned ominously around them. Rusty surgical tools were strewn across the working area. Mangled human and animal limbs lay rotting in a corner.

Sulking human skeletons hung around the room, chained to the walls for eternity as spiders clothed them in thin, white silk. On the room's far right, a crusty lab table sat in the flickering glow of the tall, green candle next to it. The angry yellow flame shed a bright, eerie light as it swatted at the air.

Morwen had to shake her head a few times to believe that everything here was real. She was not imagining a fable being told around a fire. She was not trapped in a nightmare, either. She was in a true underground fortress.

Sanguine, Morwen told herself. She suddenly regretted scaring Brynn about Tobias. In all honesty, she'd thought Tobias was a myth, and she'd twisted his fable with local concerns to spook her sister. Apparently, Sanguine was as real as the acrid stench of rotting flesh wafting from the room.

Morwen saw Brynn standing motionless in the center of the room, her back to the doorway. Her kidnapper crouched down before her and gently stroked her cheek. Morwen truly wanted to just charge into the room and save Brynn, but she was too terrified at the thought of who that dark figure probably was.

The kidnapper, facing the doorway, peered over Brynn's shoulder and pointed right at Morwen. He said in a maliciously kind tone, "Ah, look here, Brynn. We have a visitor."

Morwen, startled, turned away. She stood rigid, her back to the warm tunnel wall. Her chest rose and fell quickly. Her heart flip-flopped against her ribs. Anxiety crept over her. She closed her eyes and tried to calm herself. After regaining her composure, she opened her eyes.

Brynn's kidnapper stood in front of her. He slowly hooked a thin, black-nailed finger under her chin. He smirked, tilting his head to the side.

"Why don't you come inside?" he crooned to her. "It is much too dangerous outside for such a pretty girl like *you*."

Morwen couldn't reply.

Without moving his finger, he pulled her into the room and led her to Brynn. He lowered his hand, and Morwen regained control of herself. She dropped to her knees and hugged Brynn. She did not hug back. Brynn just stared into nothingness with glossy, white eyes.

Morwen, shaking, put both her hands on her sister's shoulders.

"What have you done to her?"

"Done what?"

"Why isn't Brynn moving?"

Brynn's captor cackled and placed his hand on Morwen's head. He stroked her hair. "Silly girl . . . Do you not know who I am?"

Morwen was almost positive that this was Tobias, but she didn't dare look up at him to prove it. "Please, give Brynn back. Now!"

"My, my, what a little temper we have here."

"Temper? But I didn't—"

"Don't worry, I can fix it," he said. He planted his foot in Morwen's back and kicked her to the floor. The entranced Brynn slid out of the way. The kidnapper walked around Morwen in a circle, buzzard-like, and then crouched down in front of her.

The Dark Wizard looked down at her with a smirk. His pale skin was yellowish and sickly, and bright crimson hair fell well past his shoulders. On each side of his face, frayed red twine and cream-colored beads bound an intricate braid together.

His slightly bent nose led down to his inflamed lips, which were slashed and striped with red scars. His harvest moon eyes, looming inside their dark-as-night sockets, watched Morwen carefully.

He grinned and held out his hand. "Hello, I am Tobias, and who are *you*?"

Morwen knew for sure now that she was not hallucinating. Tobias was real, and she and Brynn had walked right into his clutches. She did not move to grab his hand. Tobias frowned. He pulled back his hand from the rejected handshake and rested it on her cheek.

"Why so stern?" he pouted. "I am not going to bother you at all; I am more interested in *her*. Who knows what the outcome could be? She looks very promising."

Morwen jerked her face away from Tobias's hand. Her fear was melting into anger." You're not going to do *anything* to her. Give her back!"

"Why should I?"

"She's my little sister!"

Morwen stood up and threw a punch at Tobias, but the Dark Wizard grabbed her fist before it hit him. He constricted her hand in his as he came to his feet. Morwen winced when her finger bones began bending under the pressure. If he squeezed any harder, her fingers would snap in two. Tobias released Morwen and shoved her away. She flexed her fingers gratefully.

Morwen closed her eyes, taking a moment to think about what to do next. When she reopened them, she said, "Alright, I'll make you a deal."

"Oh?"

"If you let Brynn return—*safely*—back home with no recollection of this, I'll pay you a thousand gold coins in three weeks' time."

Tobias smirked, snickered, and finally broke into a full-fledged fit of cackling. He shook his head.

"I'm sorry, it's just—you're so grave, so intense!" He laughed while wiping a tear from his eye. "Your joke of a trade doesn't help your case."

Morwen, staying serious, made eye contact with him and said shakily, "*Ten* thousand, then."

Tobias laughed so hard that he was gasping for air. He stumbled toward the wall, drunk with amusement. He buried his face in his arms and pounded the wall with his fist. Finally, he started to calm down, and his breathing slowed.

His hair flushed a deeper crimson, and his skin paled before Morwen's eyes. He turned back to her, cocking his head side to side to crack his neck. He sighed. His black eye sockets became a rich, bloody red, matching his scars. Tobias calmly approached Morwen, his eyes wide with interest.

"I apologize for my—outburst. I must learn to control myself better. Well? Carry on," he said politely. His silent, hungry glare brought chills down Morwen's spine. She looked to the ground and thought.

"You know I won't trade anything for your little sister."

She looked up. "I have one last offer to give you."
"Does it involve money?" Tobias whined.
"No. It's . . . . " she said, voice trailing off.
"*Well?*"

Morwen took a deep breath in and said, "If you release Brynn safely and with no memories of this, I myself shall take her place in your experiments."

Chapter 5

"Deal."

Morwen, taken aback, asked, "*Really?*"

"Yes. Here, you can watch her leave if you like. Don't worry, I won't pull any tricks," he said. "I may come from the pits of Sanguine, but I would never dishonor myself by breaking a deal."

Morwen kneeled down by Brynn and hugged her. She whispered into her ear, "I'd never forgive myself if I let you become a monster, just remember that. I may not be the best role model ever, but I *am* your big sister, and I'll love you not matter what. I'll miss you a lot . . . "

"No, no no. Stop. Touching moments make me ill." Tobias snapped his fingers, and a nearby skeleton crackled to life and unchained itself from the wall. It approached Brynn and Morwen and stood obediently next to them. After standing up, Morwen assumed her place at Tobias's side.

The skeleton watched Tobias, awaiting a command. The Dark Wizard nodded and waved his hand in dismissal. The skeleton took Brynn's hand and led her out of the room.

Now that her mind was free of worry for Brynn, her concern now focused on herself. Her mind spun with questions. *What will happen to me now? Will I ever see my family again? Will I die?* She could not hide her worry—her entire body shivered. Tobias put his hands behind his back and paced around her, watching her. Morwen stood still, despite her knees threatening to buckle any moment.

Tobias stopped and asked, "Have you had any training in fighting?"

She nodded. "Interesting," Tobias said. "Tell me more."

"Well, I wanted to become a warrior so I could find my father. He and a few other men disappeared in a search for some lost children."

Tobias' eyebrows rose, and he smiled knowingly. "Was the search party looking for the little ones from Aren?"

"You *were* the kidnapper! Did you take my father, too?"

"Why would I care about him? I only worry about the younglings for my experiments."

"But you do know where he is."

He shrugged. "I put him and the others to good use. He's not here, though, I can tell you that."

"Tell me where he is!"

Tobias's eyes widened. "May I remind you who the master is here?" He grinned, baring his sharp yellow teeth. His skin lost all of its color, and he now glowed with a ghostly, bright white aura. His eye sockets turned black again, as did his scars.

His eyes, bloodshot, made his eager glare even more unnerving. A wide streak of white shot down his hair and spread, staining his rich red locks the color of new snow. Tobias took a step towards Morwen, and she stepped back. Again, he stepped forward, and she continued to retreat.

Morwen kept backing up as Tobias continued advancing, and he quickly backed her into a corner.

Crack! Morwen's head smacked against the wall behind her. She cringed and clutched her head, her anger throbbing as much as her skull. Tobias came even closer.

Again, Morwen tried to strike him, but his superior speed stopped the attack. He caught her wrist and did not let go. Morwen tried hurting him with her other hand and failed. Tobias squeezed her wrists and twisted them inwards. Morwen's arms and shoulders shifted uncomfortably, the joints popping and turning with Tobias's force.

Once her arms could not turn any more, her shoulders slowly started lifting from their sockets. Morwen winced and cried out, and Tobias, grinning, twisted even harder.

"STOP!" she screamed.

Tobias released her, his expression displaying just a hint of disappointment. She scowled at him as she rolled her shoulders to ease their soreness. "If you despise me so, I can always bring your sister back."

Morwen did not respond.

"I thought so. Now, girl, follow me." He turned and walked out of the room. Morwen followed. Tobias led her down the staircase leading to the heart of Sanguine. "What's your name?" he demanded.

"Excuse me?"

"What is your *name*, girl?"

"Morwen."

A streak of red flowed down his white hair, just as the white streak had earlier. The red hue spread likewise, dyeing his hair a bright crimson. He shifted back into the appearance he had when he and Morwen first met. Looking over his shoulder, he said, "I am going to place on you a special kind of spell that is called a Brand."

"A what?"

"I was looking forward to you asking that," he said. He smirked, facing ahead once again. "A Brand is a magical tattoo-like mark that the King of Sanguine places on someone to bind him—or her, in your case—to a master, whether that person be bound to a simple Underling or the King himself."

Tobias fell silent for a long while as they walked on, and Morwen stared at the back of his head expectantly. She asked carefully, "Is that all? Just a sign that I'm your servant?"

He sighed deeply and said, "*More* or less, yes."

Morwen knew Tobias was less than trustworthy. "Have you told me *everything* about it?"

Tobias stopped and faced her. Morwen stopped before she ran into him. He placed his hand on the top of her head and looked her straight in the eye.

"Now, Morwen, would I *ever* lie to you?"

"Yes."

Tobias's smile died, and he tore his hand from her head. He turned back around and continued on. Now afraid that

Tobias would kill her if she angered him further, Morwen spent the rest of the trip down the staircase in obedient silence.

When they finally reached the bottom of the staircase, a rounded doorway awaited them. The room behind it glowed menacingly with blazing oranges, reds, and yellows. Heat radiated in stifling waves from inside.

Tobias awaited her by the doorway. "Ladies first, of course."

Morwen stepped through the doorway, and Tobias snapped his fingers. Cold, invisible hands grabbed her ankles and held by the arms, lifting her off the ground. Grogs. She struggled to get free, but stopped, remembering that the creature she fought on the stairs wouldn't let go for *anything*.

Tobias approached her. "So I guess you may have met my little pet on the stairs. Most who are grabbed by a Grog end up thrashing and screaming and... it's just so enjoyable to watch."

"Is it a problem that I'm not thrashing and screaming?" she asked, raising an eyebrow.

"Why yes," he said coolly. He cackled and he turned around, his long, thick hair swishing over his shoulder. He waved his hand, ordering the Grogs to follow. Tobias led Morwen and the Grogs across a dusty stone bridge that crossed a large lake of bubbling, gurgling lava. Faint, oddly-shaped clouds of steam floated above the glowing mass of melted rock.

When Morwen squinted to get a better look at the strange haze, she saw blank, somber faces twist and sag, and their respective arms and legs dangled limply in the air. "Ghosts!" Morwen gasped.

Tobias smacked her. "Silence, girl! You're in the presence of His Majesty."

Chapter 6

Morwen snapped out of her reverie of the condemned spirits and looked ahead of her. An utterly enormous, two-story-tall man—his face hidden by his dark cloak's hood—sat silently in a shiny, black stone throne.

The gigantic chair stood about the size of a farm silo, and it was elaborately encrusted with millions of tiny, glowing orbs. Trapped spirits writhed and shrieked soundlessly inside their eternal confinements, as though begging someone to set them free. The cloaked man wore a large necklace around his neck, and from it hung a large, black, jagged key decorated with deep red rubies.

"The Key to Sanguine?" Morwen wondered aloud.

Tobias shushed her. He solemnly approached the man and knelt down on one knee, his thick curtain of hair spilling onto the dirty floor. "O Great Belial, Lord of the Dead, King of Sanguine, I wish a favor of you."

"What is it, Tobias?" King Belial bellowed with his great voice, almost shaking the ground.

"I wish to place the Brand on this young girl."

King Belial sat a little taller in his throne, and Morwen felt him stare at her through the darkness of his hood. "Ah, I see. Come."

Belial stood, almost scraping his head on the ceiling, then shrank down to be just a little taller than Tobias. He turned back to his throne, now many times taller than him.

He pulled out a lone, pearly white orb from the black rock and uncovered a small keyhole. The king took the key hanging around his neck and pushed it into the keyhole, causing a violent tremor in the floor. The ground slowly swallowed the throne, revealing a gargantuan set of redwood doors behind it.

Carvings of creatures native to Sanguine snarled and grimaced from their places on each gate. Their wooden eyes seemed to stare right at Morwen.

King Belial waved his hand at the doors, and they rumbled open. From behind them emerged a large, blue marble chamber with a lake-sized, circular pool in the middle. The clear water shimmered in the low lighting from nearby torches and rippled only slightly when the Dark King strode through the doors. Tobias and the Grogs followed close behind.

Once they all were inside, the doors slammed shut behind them with a thunderous *ka-choong*. King Belial silently pointed to the invisible Grogs, and then to the center to the pond.

They somehow understood what he wanted and took Morwen to the immense pool's center, sloshing through the water's tranquil surface. They lowered her into the water and left. Morwen stood silently, slightly confused.

"Sit down, Morwen." Tobias ordered from across the chamber.

Morwen sat, and to her surprise, she didn't get wet in the pool. She twirled her hand in the water. The liquid reacted and rippled to her movement, yet her fingers only felt a fine mist brush past them.

When she lifted her hand out of the water, her skin appeared as dry as it had been before she put it in.

"Morwen," Tobias whined, scolding her. "Stop playing. This is the sacred Pool of Bellorum. It would be wise if you showed it more respect."

Morwen scowled at Tobias and grumbled under her breath. In the blink of an eye, Tobias disappeared from the edge of the pool. Morwen sensed someone sitting to her right, and she noticed Tobias's face next to hers.

She jumped and gasped at his sudden company. His long hair had become an electrifying white, his eye sockets and scars were jet black. His skin glowed white while his eyes were wide open, bloodshot. He smiled from ear to ear and breathed shallowly, letting out a single high-pitched giggle or two as he exhaled. Morwen's breathing sped up, her heart quivered, and her limbs fell weak.

"Embarrass me in front of the King," he threatened in a shrill, raspy voice. "And I'll hang you from the gallows with a rope of your own hair!"

A wave of tingling chills rushed down Morwen's body as she whimpered and nodded quickly. When she looked back up at Tobias, his features were normal again.

He grinned happily and said loud enough for King Belial to hear, "Now that I've settled that, let's continue. Your Majesty? Could you please begin?"

"With pleasure."

Tobias appeared back at the King's side.

The King produced a large, gnarled cherry-wood staff—topped off with a human skull—from the palm of his hand. He stepped to the edge of the pool and stabbed the water with it. As if he had speared a fish through the heart, blood rose from below the staff and spread throughout the pool.

Morwen, paralyzed in fear, watched as the clear water around her thickened into blood.

King Belial drew a glittering, diamond-bladed dagger from his robe pocket and handed it to Tobias. Tobias took the dagger and slit his own throat. Black blood sprayed from his neck.

The dark dagger—Tobias was completely unharmed, though. Immortals like him could do almost anything to themselves without dying. Tobias bent over, cupping his bleeding neck in one hand, and approached the pool. Leaning over the scarlet water, he let his blood gush into the pool.

As the ripples from his blood droplets echoed throughout the water, so did the blood's color. Before Morwen knew it, the entire Pool of Bellorum was cloaked in a thick shroud of black.

After the color evenly spread around, the liquid surrounding Morwen bubbled and shiver as if boiling. The bubbles slowly migrated towards her. For only a moment did she consider letting Tobias take Brynn back. But she remained strong.

The bubbles surrounded her and burst, their black pigment splattering all over her. The black color silently slithered to her right arm, and soon to the top of her arm. It stopped at her deltoid muscle. The black stain hissed like acid and dove into her skin.

The pain of a trillion pieces of parchment carefully but quickly slit her skin in every direction. She flinched, eyes tearing up. She longed to scream, but she feared Tobias's death threat.

The dark coloring swirled in a circular motion under her skin, halted, and oozed into a bizarre shape. Morwen looked down to see a tattoo-like mark had just formed on her skin.

A black sun looked up at her with a skull—colored with her own skin tone—in its center. The rays of the sun reached outward from the skull. Their tips melted into a black ring encircling that sun.

The bottom of the ring had a small opening at the bottom, which allowed the bottom sunray to become short and pointed, like a bee stinger awaiting its first victim. The two bottom sides of the mark's opening dripped into two parallel spikes resembling hummingbird beaks.

After the pigment finished moving, Morwen glanced at the intricate Brand. Maddening shrieks that rang in her ears. She covered her ears with her hands, trying to block out the almost ear-shattering racket.

Her efforts in vain. Nothing could stop the din that clawed at her eardrums. She shook her head back and forth to make the screeching stop, and she looked at Tobias and King Belial across the chamber. They seemed unaffected by the uproar. They both stood there calmly, watching her reaction to the Brand.

"Can't you hear it, too?" Morwen cried.

Tobias cocked his head and asked in almost faked confusion, "What? Hear what?"

Strangely, Morwen could hear Tobias very clearly through the racket, as though he was standing next to her.

"Can't you hear the shrieking? It's deafening!" She continued to cover her ears.

"Oh, you mean the screams of the souls down here? I seem to have gotten used to it over my year here. I can't really hear it at all anymore."

"Then why can *I* hear it? I couldn't hear it before."

Tobias rolled his eyes, a grin spreading across his face. "Did I tell you? *Silly* me! Morwen," he smirked as he suddenly appeared in front of her, kneeling down to meet her face. "Only immortals like the king and me can hear that noise. Are you *sure* can hear it?"

"Stop joking around! Wait . . . oh, no. Do you mean—?"

"Mean what?"

"Mean that . . . . "

Before Morwen could finish, all the muscles in her arm tensed and shook as if in a seizure. Her arm stung from what seemed like a thousand butcher knives slicing into the skin around her Brand.

Her arm twisted and turned wildly, but she used her left hand to steady it. Morwen couldn't take it anymore. Her cries of pain and agony joined those surrounding her. Tears raced down her cheeks as her right arm danced out of her incredibly tight grip.

A great bout of dizziness hit Morwen. Her vision blurred, and she swayed from side to side in the pool. She squinted upward at Tobias, just a red and black blur. He waved cheerfully at her as if nothing was wrong. Everything went black, and Morwen felt the thin, chilly sensation from the pool cushion her face.

Tobias's voice echoed through the darkness, "Oh, and I forgot to tell you . . . the Brand will spread across your body, and when it swallows you whole, you'll be transformed into a puppet to use at *my* disposal."

He cackled maliciously, and then . . . silence.

Chapter 7

Morwen shot upright, leaving a puddle of icy sweat soaking her pillow. Her gaze flew around the room, fearful that Tobias was nearby. Evening sunshine spilled through a western window. She was at her home. She was safe and far away from Tobias's grasp. Sinking down into her covers, she smiled and put her hand on her forehead.

I must have taken a nap after we came back from town. Tobias was just a bad dream.

She sighed as her fear faded away. "That might've been the worst one yet." She had suffered terrible dreams ever since her father's disappearance.

Morwen couldn't resist checking her right sleeve, which had ripped off in her "nightmare." The sleeve was still in place—but just barely.

A thick black thread held the cloth where it met the shoulder of her shirt. Still desperately trying to deny her experience, Morwen slid out of bed and walked towards the door of her room, which was hidden around the corner from her bed. She stepped around the corner and gasped, covering her mouth.

Her bedroom door dripped with a thick, red liquid. Morwen squinted at it and managed to read the ominous message: *Tell anyone about it, and you'll take responsibility for your family's murder.*

Morwen gasped. Her hand flew to her right arm. Fingers shaking, she pulled up her long leather sleeve. She found the Brand and shivered. This parasite of a curse was under her skin, waiting for the best moment to start spreading its wrath.

So it was all real. I guess it won't be long before this thing eats me alive.

Morwen paced around her room. Her head spun. She had scared Brynn about a villain thought to only live in fables, but he actually *did* exist. Morwen had traded her future to him. The proof was on her right arm.

Was she supposed to be filled with terror? Fury? Agony? All of those emotions gripped her at the same time. Her breath quickened, and she paced more quickly, growing dizzy. She sank to the floor. "What have I done?" She rolled up her sleeve and looked at the Brand again.

"*What have I done?*" She threw her hands into the air. "I'll become the servant of a dark wizard with a vendetta."

Morwen's heart sank. She wanted to hide under her bed and let herself rot. Her stomach growled. She stood carefully, her body still rattling with all the thoughts of her horrible future. Morwen steadied herself on the wall and inched to her door. The message had disappeared. *Good,* Morwen thought. *Now Mother or Brynn won't find it.*

Morwen *ka-lumped* down the stairs and saw her mother and sister eating dinner at the table.

Mother scowled up at her daughter. "Why did you leave Brynn by the woods and come home without her? Were you that desperate for a nap?"

Morwen's mind tried to fabricate a believable—and *safe*—answer. She kept the message on the door fresh in her mind. "I was playing at the edge of the woods with Brynn when a white rabbit came by, and I wanted to chase it. She stayed behind, but I—um—followed it for awhile and got lost. I was so tired that once I found my way home I just collapsed."

Mother frowned. Morwen's stomach tightened. *Oh, no. She doesn't believe me.*

"You deliberately went into the forest after I told you not to? You had better not even get near there *ever* again, or you will find yourself in more trouble than you can handle."

"I understand."

After a long, angry silence, Mother sighed. "Well, you must be hungry after all your walking. I'll make you dinner."

Morwen sat down at the table. Mother went to the stove. Morwen shook her head while she stared at the tabletop, thinking. *How could she possibly have believed my answer? I guess the message was a spell to help me hide what happened, including the Brand.*

Mother set a plate piled high with corn and boar meat in front of Morwen. Suddenly, the Brand began stinging as if a salty finger was peeling off her skin. She winced and held her arm.

"Are you alright?" Mother asked.

Morwen thought quickly. "Will you excuse me for a moment?"

Brynn giggled. Morwen rushed to the washroom upstairs. She slammed the door shut and turned to an oblong, oak-framed mirror. She rolled up her shirt's sleeve and found the Brand had changed. Shiny, bright, turquoise scales replaced the dark blood ink.

"It's growing," she told her reflection. "I need to find someone who can get this thing off me." *But who could possibly do that?*

"Armando!" Morwen rushed downstairs to the front door.

"Morwen," Mother called from the kitchen. "Please clean your dishes before you go chasing boys."

"I don't *chase boys*," Morwen retorted. "I . . . . "

She paused. "Alright, I confess. I like to sneak out of the house to spy on the Erikson boys in the glade."

Mother walked out of the kitchen, smiling. "I remember spying on boys when I was your age. I was so obsessed with boys at the time that I would actually climb out my bedroom window in the dead of night to watch them."

She faked a smile. "That's . . . very interesting! So after I clean my dishes, may I go?"

"Absolutely."

Morwen ran back to the table to retrieve her clay plate and cup. She pushed all the food and crumbs off her dishes, then waved goodbye to her mother while hurrying to the door. She was about to leave the cottage when she heard a small, high-pitched voice speak behind her. She turned around and saw Brynn looking up at her with her wide, bright, blue eyes.

"I hope you find a handsome knight out there, Morwen," Brynn peeped with an innocent smile.

Morwen bent down and gave Brynn a big hug, then whispered, "Of course. And I'll tell you all about it when I return."

Brynn nodded and broke free of the hug, running back to the kitchen to help finish washing the dishes. Morwen hurried away.

It was the ideal summer evening in Aren. The town's unique air was fresh enough to cleanse the sickest of lungs, and the crisp aroma from the surrounding pine trees tickled the throat.

The orchestras of crickets lulled the town to sleep with a symphony of clicks and chirps in time to the fireflies' gentle flickering in the approaching darkness. The moon was a thin crescent in the indigo sky rimmed with magenta. The stars speckled the sky with their brilliance.

Morwen noticed little of the serene beauty as she ran to Armando's hut at the edge of the woods. When she arrived, she knocked on the heavy wooden door and heard loud scuffling inside.

"Who is it?" Armando asked gruffly.

"Morwen."

"You know you shouldn't come to my hut. We only meet for training near the forest. *In secret.*"

"But it's an emergency!"

"I am not teaching you anything right now. Go home."

"It's about a curse put on me! If you let me in, I'll show you."

Armando opened the door and waved his hand. "Quickly."

Morwen stepped into his hut. His furnishings consisted of a worn brown hammock, a chest, a table and three chairs, and a fireplace. Numerous candles dotted the room, shedding a dim, flickering light upon the simple interior.

Armando ushered Morwen to the table, and she sat down. "You're shivering," he said worriedly. "Rest a moment." He hurried to the fireplace and grabbed a black iron kettle, bringing it to the table and filling a large mug with steaming-hot tea. Then he settled in a chair with a raspy groan—his knees were getting worse.

She sipped the tea, and her shivering ceased.

He asked kindly, "Now Morwen, what is it? What's wrong?"

Morwen opened her mouth to speak, but she shut it, trying to find a way to tell him about the Brand without saying it outright. She did not want Tobias's threat on her door to come true. Suddenly, she got an idea.

"Could you please tell me what *this* is? I don't know what it could be." She pulled up her right shirt sleeve.

Armando gazed at the scaly Brand on her arm, his face blank and solemn. "Does it hurt?"

"Yes."

He touched the scales on her arm. "Was this pattern black when you first got it?"

She nodded.

"Who did this to you?"

"I—I don't know. He hid his face."

Armando sat up taller in his chair and took his hand off Morwen's arm. The look in his gray eyes scared her.

"Morwen, what you've got here is a demonic tattoo called a Brand. Basically, whoever gets this mark is branded as 'property' of a certain demonic being or dark user of magic. It ends up spreading across a person's body in an extremely painful manner, as you may have started experiencing.

If it completely engulfs your body, you'll be transformed into a powerful, immortal creature and will become the servant—the slave—of your master. You will still be the same person when transformed, but will be under complete influence of your master."

She tried to stay calm. "So . . . the Brand swallows up my body and free will?"

The Branding

"Not quite. It may appear that it's only spreading across your skin, but the enchantment on it seeps into you... and eventually swallows your soul, taking control of all your body systems on its way there."

Terror crept over Morwen. "Do you have a spell to take it off?"

Armando sighed again. He looked miserable. "I'm sorry Morwen, the Brand is much too powerful for an old adventurer like me."

Morwen's heart sank, and tears blurred her sight. She buried her face in her arms. Armando scooted his chair closer to hers and wrapped his arms around his young student in comfort.

She turned and hugged him back, sobbing into his rough shirt. Armando had become a second father to Morwen. Though he did not know it, he'd helped her cope with her real father's absence.

"I *don't* want this to happen to me, Armando."

"Morwen, don't surrender yet. There is some hope."

"Like what?"

"There is one person powerful enough to take the Brand off you. His name is Kain. He's a Master wizard whose power is second only to King Dragomir's. If you find him, he'll surely be able to help you."

Morwen pulled away from the hug and asked, a bit of hope in her voice, "Where does he live? I must get the Brand off of me as soon as possible!"

Armando gave her a small, sorrowful smile. "He lives on the top of Mt. Schism, in his castle of white marble."

Morwen shot up from her chair, knocking it to the floor. "But that's all the way across the country from here!"

He nodded.

"Master Armando, I can't go *alone!* Will you go with me, please?"

"I am getting much too old for travel. You can handle yourself. I know you can. I would only slow you down."

"Oh, but you could just—" Morwen cringed as the Brand gave her another dose of stinging pain, although it didn't spread.

Armando shook his head and sighed once again, becoming sadder and sadder as Morwen's situation grew worse by the minute. Yet his decision was made. "You will leave tonight," he said firmly.

Chapter 8

"*Tonight?*" Morwen gasped. "Can't I at least go home to pack my things? To say my goodbyes?"

"No. You must not speak to anyone. You have to leave at once."

"But please let me go home one last time. I might never see Mother and Brynn again!"

Armando sighed. "Fine. But be vigilant. Do not be seen by anyone, do you understand?"

Morwen nodded and hugged Armando again. "Thank you."

She stumbled out of the hut and into the night. This was hardly the ideal adventure of her dreams.

The crescent moon was still high in the sky, and the stars were still as bright. The crickets continued to chirp their joyous song, and the frogs had joined in with their choirs of squeaks and croaks. In the distance, Morwen heard the wolves howl remorsefully to each other as the owls greeted the flickering fireflies with loud, long hoots.

All of these familiar night sounds were comforting and welcoming, but her odd gut feeling kept her alert.

She slowly, cautiously, walked down the main road in Aren. She heard the thump of footsteps behind her. When she stopped to look, the footsteps stopped, too. She turned back around and walked a little faster, and the sound of the footsteps followed suit.

I've got to get home . . . quickly.

She turned onto the side road that led to the Aleacim cottage. The footsteps behind her grew louder now, and she sprinted for the safety of home. She tripped over a rock, and a pair of strong arms caught her from behind.

Those arms snaked around her, and a low, familiar voice cooed in her ear, "Hello, Morwen."

"Syltas."

Syltas pulled Morwen's body closer to his. "Why are you outdoors at such a time as this?" He brought her so close she could feel his heartbeat against her back.

"Let me go, or I will have to force my way free," Morwen said.

Syltas buried his face in her hair. "I apologize. I can't help it, really. You're just so *beautiful*."

Again, Morwen tried to break free from him, but Syltas kept a firm hold on her. "Stop. I mean it."

"Morwen, do you wish to accompany me to the creek, like I said this morning?"

"No. Now let . . . me . . . go!"

She squirmed. Syltas covered her mouth with his hand. She bit one of his fingers. He cried out but didn't let go. "If I cannot have you, then no one else should."

He let go of her mouth and unsheathed a butcher's knife from his belt—probably stolen from the pork seller down the road. He pressed the blade against her throat.

Morwen swallowed hard.

Syltas nudged her forward, still applying pressure to the knife. He forced her into the woods with him and stopped when they came to a clearing. As he removed the knife from her throat, he shoved her to the ground.

Syltas crouched down next to her and brandished the butcher knife again. He brought his face closer to Morwen's, and she spat at him. He pinched her chin and pulled her closer to him so they were almost nose-to-nose.

"Leave me alone!" she screeched. Her right hand flew to Syltas's throat.

"Ooh, physical threats, now?" he asked. "You won't be as intimidating once your pretty face is clean off your head!"

Suddenly, the Brand stung again, and she felt it slowly crawl a few inches down her upper arm. As the pain from the Brand increased, her hand closed tighter on Syltas's throat. He pulled her into a rough kiss. Her hand constricted on his neck even tighter during the kiss, and now she could feel the quickening pulse of his vein.

Sytlas made an awful gurgling sound. She pulled away. His eyes stared at her, wide in fear. He swallowed hard, and his chest heaved.

"Stop," he choked, dropping his weapon. "This isn't funny. Stop."

The Brand throbbed even harder as her hand squeezed his throat tighter.

Syltas started wheezing, his eyes crossing in desperation for breath. He slumped to the ground next to her, her hand still strangling him. "Please, Morwen," he managed to say. "Have mercy. I—I'll leave you alone! Just let me go . . . "

Morwen tried to release her grip, but couldn't, no matter how hard she struggled. Against her will, her hand's hold on Syltas's neck grew tighter than ever as her Brand burned and stung and continued to slither down her arm.

She felt Syltas's neck bones crackle and snap as her hand closed all the way around his throat.

He wailed and pleaded through a torrent of tears. "Stop! Stop! Morwen, please stop! Help! Someone, HEEELP!! PLEEASE!!!"

"I'm sorry! I can't let go! It won't stop!"

Syltas's shouting stopped. He went limp. A still, sickening silence fell upon the woods. The crickets stopped chirping, the frogs retreated under the surface of their shallow ponds, and the owls buried their beaks in their wings.

Morwen shut her eyes in fear of what she would see as her hand slowly closed into a fist. A warm liquid flowed onto her hand, and a jagged, hard object poked out from between her fingers. The air filled with the faint aroma of copper. Morwen sniffed through petrified tears. A short popping noise and a soft hissing broke the silence as the warm liquid misted onto her face. Morwen opened her eyes, and her heart stopped. She opened her mouth and produced an ear-shattering scream that shook woods for miles around.

Chapter 9

She had ripped out Syltas's throat.

Morwen shot to her feet, taking one last glance at his glossy eyes. She turned and sprinted back to Armando's hut. She threw herself at his door, pounding it with all her might.

Armando opened the door quickly, and Morwen fell onto the ground in front of him, her right arm soaked in blood. She curled into a ball at his feet, hysterical and shaking. Armando quickly scooped her into his arms and laid her in his hammock, shutting the heavy door behind him with his foot. He tore off a piece of his sleeve, dunking it in a bucket of cold water. He gently wiped the blood from Morwen's face.

She calmed down quickly, though she still shook a little as blood dripped off her right arm. "Master Armando?"

"Yes?"

"I am so very, *very* sorry!"

"For what?" he asked in a low, caring voice. "Well, just wait one minute. I'll clean up your arm."

Armando brought the bucket of his planned-to-be-soup water and a chair over to the hammock. He sat down next to her. He took her right arm and dipped it into the cool liquid, watching the blood ooze into the water and tint it red.

"What happened?" he asked finally.

"I—I—I killed someone! I couldn't help it! The Brand took over me! I killed Syltas!"

"Shhh, shhh. It's alright. Be thankful that your Brand didn't spread more than it has."

"Once the elders find his body, I'll be kicked out of Aren—if I'm not executed first."

"Then, as I said, you must leave as soon as possible. I for one would choose exile over execution."

Morwen also preferred isolation over death, but leaving Mother, Brynn and Armando would kill her inside. Not to mention that she'd go mad if she discovered that Tobias had lied about her father, and he returned home in her absence.

"Is there any hope of me staying here?" she asked Armando.

He shook his head. "No, none at all."

She could never sleep in her safe, soft bed again, nor could she dance in the morning sunlight on the cottage doorstep. She wouldn't experience the lovely aromas of the market or chat with neighbors on warm evenings.

She wouldn't ever play with Brynn on days she was not a pest, nor could she ever confide in her mother again. The cozy life she had once wished so desperately to abandon now called to her with every beat of her heart.

But she, Morwen Aleacim, was now an outcast, an exile. She now knew that her old life had officially ended.

The Brand flared up again. She cried out. An invisible torturer seemed to peel her flesh off and sew it back on with brambles and rusted needles. The water in the bucket splashed all over the floor as her arm squirmed from the slow transformation.

Armando watched grimly, patting her shoulder.

Just as suddenly as it had started, the pain stopped, and Morwen, exhausted, rested her head on the hammock pillow. She pulled her arm out of the water and held it up in front of her face. She gasped.

Her arm had become a shiny, turquoise-scaled limb with inch-long black claws. The scaly fingers closed into a fist and back out into a flat hand.

Worried, she looked up at Armando, who rested his hand on her scaly one.

"Morwen," he said calmly. "Since the Brand has been so active, it will stay somewhat dormant and not spread for about a week or so, but it will still have control over this arm, now that it has completely covered it."

"I can't go out into the world with this *thing* on me!"

Armando went to his chest by the dinner table, unlatched it, and pulled out a thick hawking glove. He handed it to Morwen, and she slipped it over her right hand.

He smiled a little. "See? It looks completely normal now."

"I have to leave now, don't I?"

"Yes, child."

"I have no supplies."

"Don't worry, you can take some of my things." He pointed to a cowhide satchel by his feet. "I keep my bread and water in there." Armando hobbled to his chest again and pulled out a small sword and a wooden stake. He came back to Morwen and set the weaponry by the satchel. "The silver shortsword. Good for fighting off creatures of darkness."

"But what about the wooden stake?"

"It's for you."

Stunned and sure that she had heard him wrong, Morwen asked, "*What* is it for?"

"Even though the Brand has lots of negative effects on you—like eating your soul—it has one positive aspect. It makes you almost invincible. *Almost.* Whether someone slices your arm off or slits your throat, you'll still live. You'll just regenerate the limb or heal the wound."

"*Almost* invincible? Then what can hurt me? The stake?"

"Yes, but please let me finish. The Brand makes you invincible to ensure you won't kill yourself to escape from it before it takes you over. It's also a sign that you're on your way to becoming an immortal like your master.

If you don't make it in time to Kain's castle, Morwen, you must drive this very stake into your heart. That's the only vulnerable spot." He hesitated, then added quietly, "The only way you can escape this curse is by dying like that."

Morwen looked down at the stake. She shuddered at the thought that it might kill her in the future.

Armando set a hand on her head in reassurance. "Don't worry. I doubt you'll ever have to use it. I have a map that shows the quickest way to Kain. Here." He pulled a wrinkled piece of parchment from his shirt. "I'm just giving you the stake as a necessary precaution. I wish I could accompany you, honestly, but I am not an energetic young man anymore. I would slow you down too much, and then you would never get to Kain in time."

Morwen slid out of the hammock. She took the map and stuffed it into a pocket of her pants. She slung the cowhide bag onto her back and tied the shortsword, safe in its sheath, to her belt.

Armando saw the stake still on the floor, and picking it up, he dropped it into Morwen's bag. "It's just a precaution," he repeated.

"I guess this is goodbye, then. Forever."

"No. Not goodbye, not forever. Good luck, Morwen." Armando hugged her tightly. He took a deep breath and added, "You'll make it in time. I have taught you well, and I *know* you are a brave warrior. You can handle yourself."

Morwen fought back tears. "I'm going to miss you and Brynn and my mother so much."

"I'll miss you, also. And I'm sure your family will never forget about you. I'll see if I can come up with some likely explanation that may help them cope. Now go. Before dawn breaks."

Morwen walked slowly to the door. She opened it wide, and the warm evening air drifted across her face. She turned around and waved goodbye.

Armando smiled, nodded, and sat back down in his seat.

Morwen shut the door behind her and ran down the main street of Aren. She pulled the map out of her pocket as she moved through the silent village. There was enough moonlight to show the direction she had to go: due north. She folded the map up and slid it back into her pocket.

She stopped just once and looked towards her family's cottage. Her heart ached to say goodbye to her family, to talk to them one last time, but she knew she couldn't. She glanced down at her gloved right hand, then turned away from her home.

She hurried out of Aren and into the Silvia Forest.

Morwen ventured through the woods for about an hour, occasionally peeking at her map to see if she was still on the right path. When she passed an enormous oak tree, the bushes rustled behind her. She whipped around and quickly set her hand on her sword's hilt, ready to fight.

The bushes moved even more, and a doe and her fawn jumped out. They both stared at Morwen, staying as still to keep her from advancing on them. She didn't want to upset or scare the deer, so she walked onward without paying them any more attention.

After a long while, Morwen stopped by a shriveled tree stump and sat, gratefully resting her tired legs. She forced herself to look at her gloved hand.

Well, since there's no one around, I'm taking this off.

Morwen pinched the middle finger of the glove and started to slip it off, but suddenly something flew toward her from a tree about ten feet away. It smacked her hard in the forehead, knocking her backwards off the stump.

Dazed, Morwen moved weakly, shakily. Twigs snapped on the ground near her, and the noise grew louder each second. Whatever it was, it was making its stealthy way to her. She looked up and stared upward. A cloaked figure stood over her in the darkness of the woods.

A low male voice cried from under its hood, "*Sweet Mother of Dragomir*, I killed her!"

Morwen sat up, holding her throbbing head. "No, really, I'm fine . . ."

The hooded man scooped Morwen up into his arms. He ran with her through the woods as quickly as a horse, nimbly leaping over logs and dodging trees.

"*What* are you *doing* with me?" Morwen demanded through the whistling of the branches.

"Saving your life!"

"I do not need any saving! Please, find your damsel in distress somewhere else!"

"If you don't get help in time, you'll *die*!"

Thinking he was referencing to her Brand, Morwen retorted hotly, "Yes, I know! So go away!"

The hooded man shook his head and said, exasperated, "I don't understand you villagers sometimes . . . " He tripped over a gnarled tree root and fell.

Morwen flew from his arms and landed before him. She scrambled to her feet and dusted herself off. The hooded man leapt up and charged towards her, but he tripped over another root from the same tree and fell against her, knocking her to the ground again.

"You *pervert!*" Morwen snapped as she shoved him. He was lying directly on top of her.

"I—I'm sorry. I—I just can't see where I'm going—I'm very sorry." He rolled away from her.

Morwen stood up yet again. Moonlight managed to break through numerous trees' branches. Something dangled in front of her eyes. An arrow. It protruded from her head like a bug's antenna. So that's what had smacked her in the face.

"You s-shot me!" she cried. Morwen tugged, and the arrow came out with a sickening crackling noise. A familiar, warm liquid dripped down her face. "See? I'm fiiiine," she bragged, dizzy with the thought that she'd just pulled an arrow from her own skull. She drunkenly stumbled away and lost her already weak balance. She easily fell over.

The hooded man ran over to her, picked her up again, and sprinted through the woods. "You're 'fine'? Sure you are. I'm helping you out whether you like it or not!"

Morwen wanted to argue, but she lost consciousness from her bleeding before she could utter one word.

Chapter 10

Alan Saratogas slid the bloody, unconscious elf onto his bed, then darted to his chest of drawers to retrieve bandages for her. He flung his black-hooded cloak onto the small, round dinner table in his one-room cottage.

He pulled up a chair next to the girl, sat down, and wiped her face clean with his black shirt sleeve. Next he snatched a small, corked bottle of medicine from under the bed and opened it. He dipped his strong fingers into the sticky mixture and spread it over the arrow wound. He carefully wrapped bandages around her head.

Alan walked over to his dinner table and sank into a chair, rubbing a hand over his pointed ears. He was a very young man, only eighteen elf years old. He cradled his head in his hand and watched her in remorse.

He had almost killed her, an innocent girl who appeared to be only a little younger than himself, all because he wanted that large buck he saw earlier that night.

He sighed. The girl's soft, pine-green hair flowed down her shoulders and chest. Her fair skin glowed with youth. Her lips were pink and full, framed by her smooth face and pointed ears. Alan gazed at her blankly.

As he looked her over from head to toe and back again, something caught his eye: the leather glove about to slide off her right hand.

Taking care to not wake her, he snuck over and reached for the glove. The girl breathed in deeply, and Alan froze. She exhaled, and he grabbed her glove. He slowly pulled it off, knowing very well that it was rude to pry. When he saw what the glove was hiding, he gasped and backed away quickly, almost knocking over a nearby chair. Shiny scales completely covered the girl's right arm. And she had *claws*.

"So the flower has thorns," Alan muttered. He dropped the glove on the bed and snuck back to the table to watch her again. Right as he sat down, the girl stirred and opened her eyes.

Alan rushed to her side.

Morwen blinked. As her vision cleared, she saw a lanky woodland elf standing over her. His bronze hair fell over one shoulder in a tight braid. He was quite handsome, but Morwen was unsure why she was in his hut. She sat up in the bed.

He bowed politely and looked up at her from beneath his brows. His braid swung gently. "Hello, my name is Alan Saratogas."

Morwen, while somewhat enchanted by his great politeness and handsome features, still kept her guard up. "Um, I'm Morwen. Morwen Aleacim. Why am I here?"

Alan smiled and chuckled. "Do you remember that hooded man in the forest?"

Morwen thought for a moment. "That was *you*? You shot me in the head!"

"I promise you, it was an accident. I'm very sorry," He said, blushing. Alan shifted from foot to foot in his hide pants and leather boots. He cleared his throat and wiped his brow.

Morwen glared at him. "I'm used to boys acting badly when the adults are gone, but none of them ever shot me with an arrow."

"I am *so* sorry. But I assure you, I am nothing like those perverted nayhogs."

"I never thought you were." She blurted out those words, surprising herself.

Alan smiled. He sat down next to the bed and glanced at Morwen's hand.

Morwen gasped. "Where did my glove go?" She found it on the bed and slid it onto her hand.

Alan tried to look casual. "If you don't mind me asking, what happened to your hand?"

"I—er—have a curse on me that will spread along my body like a rash, and if I don't get it taken off in time, I'll... die." She wouldn't risk telling him anything more specific about the Brand.

"So that's why you're wandering alone in the woods?"

"Yes." She pulled out the map and pointed to Kain's castle. "And I have to travel *there* before I get too—infected."

Alan studied the map. "I can help you, if you don't mind my company."

"I appreciate that you want to help, but I am a warrior-in-training. I can handle all the beasts in the woods—except, perhaps, bad archers who use me as a target."

His brows arched. "You train in combat despite the laws against it?"

"Yes."

Alan snorted. "I thought the emperor's laws were meant to control ambitious girls like you."

"One day all girls will be trained to wield a weapon as well as I can." She couldn't resist adding, "And they won't shoot unsuspecting people in the head."

"I can handle a bow quite skillfully, you know," Alan countered. "Granted, I had but a few years of my father's training before he died. I've learned to read maps well, too. I'm a woodsman. You know, my skills could truly come in handy for you."

"Sorry, Alan, but I cannot have anyone come with me. I can be quite... *dangerous* at times. If you were around, there's a great possibility that I could end up, well, killing you."

Alan looked her straight in the eye. "That's a chance I am willing to take."

Morwen rolled her eyes. "Honestly, why do you want to join me?"

Alan said, "My father—he was killed by a pack of fire hounds when I was thirteen. He was a fantastic archer, you know, and he was my hero. He still is, actually. I went on hunting trips with him so I could learn how to be as great as he was. I wanted to follow right in his footsteps no matter what I had to do."

"And what about your mother?"

"She went into hysterics when she heard the news of his death. After his burial, she said she wanted to spend a few days away from home to clear her mind, but she never returned."

Morwen asked carefully, "Does that mean she's dead, also?"

"I don't know."

"But why do you insist on coming with me when your mother might return when you're gone?"

His shoulders sank. "I don't really expect her to come back."

Morwen stifled an urge to pat him on the arm. "I see."

"By joining you on your quest, I can gain experience on unfamiliar land and become a truly skilled archer. I want to make my father proud, but I am not doing so well by running in the woods around *here* every day."

Morwen thought for a moment. "If you absolutely insist, you may join me, but I warn you again: I can be extremely dangerous at times."

Alan laughed. "When are things in this world not perilous?"

"True. Then we can leave as soon as you've packed your things."

He stood up and bowed with a smile. "As you wish."

Alan hurried over to a beaten oak trunk across the cottage. He pulled out an enormous leather hunting bag and set it next to him. He visited other parts of the house and retrieved flasks of water, a loaf of bread, his worn longbow, a full quiver of arrows, and an armful of clothes. When he had gotten his supplies, he shoved them all—save his bow and arrows—into his bag and tied it shut.

Morwen slid off the bed and stood up. She stretched her tight muscles while Alan donned his bag, quiver and black traveling cloak. He held his bow in his hand.

He walked over to Morwen and glanced at her sword. "Are you sure you want to walk around with that heavy sword on your belt? I could carry it for you."

"No thanks. I'm quite capable."

"As you wish."

"Let's get going. We have a long way to go and little time to get there."

Morwen walked towards the door.

Alan rushed ahead of her and opened it for her. Once she left his hut, Alan shut his front door and locked it up tight behind him. The darkness closed around them. "How's your head, Morwen?"

"Oh, I'm sure it's fine; it'll probably heal in the next day or so," she lied, remembering that she could easily heal her own wounds. "So . . . in which direction do we need to go? I've been heading north."

"If you give me the map, I'll be able to show you."

Morwen pulled the map out of her pocket and handed it to Alan, who opened it and squinted at it through the moonlight. Though elves' pointed ears gave them superior hearing, their sight was just as weak as a human's.

"We continue due north. We can follow the Tundra Star until we get to Terra's Hollow. I've been there before when I was little. It will take us about three hours to arrive if we walk—and don't run into any trouble. And by the way, do you mind if *I* carry the map?"

"I suppose. I don't know that much about navigating."

Alan shoved the map into his pocket and looked up at the sky again. He spotted the bright twinkle of the Tundra Star and pointed at it. Morwen walked briskly in its direction. Alan watched her from behind.

He laughed to himself and ran to catch up. "Won't you wait for me?"

"I will if you get too far behind, but it makes me anxious to waste even a minute with my—problem. Besides, you've certainly demonstrated that you can run quickly when you need to. You should be able to keep up with me."

Alan shook his head. "Morwen, I have never met a young woman like you."

"Oh really?"

"Don't take it offensively. I mean that your willingness to take chances and break rules is very rare for a girl."

"Thank you, then."

Two-and-a-half quiet hours passed—an eternity in Morwen's mind. At last, the forest's trees stopped and opened up to a vast green field. The flowing plain of ankle-high grass stretched into the dark horizon. A tiny, glowing dot loomed right where the sky and earth met.

"That is Terra's Hollow," said Alan. "It'll be difficult to get over there, though."

"Why? It's just a large field. What could be wrong with it?"

"It's cursed. This field is an ancient battleground, and one of the generals in that battle prayed in his dying breath that his enemies would never desecrate his tribe's land again.

Because of his last wish, if anything or anyone steps on the battleground, corpses and spirits of his warriors come back to life and defend their leader's land. The only thing that puts the undead soldiers back to rest is if that someone or something who stepped on the land enters Terra's Hollow."

"So how are we going to get from here to Terra's Hollow?"

"We'll run like hell."

Morwen swallowed hard. "We're actually going *through* the field?"

"Yes, and so we don't get separated, we'll . . . need to hold hands," Alan said as he slipped Morwen's soft hand into his. Morwen held on tightly.

"Are you ready?" Alan asked.

"Are you sure we won't be outnumbered when we are attacked?"

"Trust me." He squeezed her hand. "I have gone through this before. Run on three, alright? One . . . two . . . three!"

Alan and Morwen sped off into the field as quickly as their feet could carry them. Suddenly, the ground rumbled under them, and they heard the sharp crackling of dirt being unturned around them.

Morwen looked over her shoulder as she ran and saw skinny, shriveled arms bursting from the ground and specters materializing in the air. Morwen turned back around and ran even harder.

The dead soldiers croaked and groaned behind Alan and Morwen. The warm summer night's air chilled around them, and Morwen and Alan's breath became white, misty clouds coming from their noses and mouths.

The phantoms flew next to them and reached out with long-nailed fingers. Morwen looked behind herself again and saw a seemingly infinite army of mutilated, moldy soldier corpses gaining on them.

"Alan, they're getting closer!"

"We have got a ways to go before we reach the town. We *have* to stay focused."

"I know that, but I do not know how much longer I can run!" Morwen heard the *ka-thumping* of hooves from behind.

Alan looked behind them, and his eyes widened. He pounced on Morwen and pulled her close to the ground. A large, three-legged horse—one leg looked to have been sliced off during battle—with a bare-chested rider leaped over them. The horse came to a halt a few feet away from Alan and Morwen.

Alan looked up at its rider, and his face grew pale. "Th— That's the general I told you about, Morwen." Alan came to his feet and pulled her up in the process, seeing that the zombies were only a mere twenty feet away from them and still approaching quickly.

The general's bony face was covered in gray, slashed skin accented with squirming maggots. His left eyeball hung down his face, and his white hair flowed down to his waist. He did not look like he died at a very old age, but it was hard to tell for sure. His horse's body, a pale indigo, was striped with battle scars and dotted with missing pockets of flesh. The animal leered at Morwen and Alan with its bright yellow eyes. Moss and mushrooms clumped in its tail and mane.

"Morwen," Alan whispered again.

"Yes?"

"When I distract him, we'll run as fast as we can to the town, alright? No looking back."

"Right."

Alan gasped loudly and shouted as he turned around pointed above the approaching zombie horde, "We are all doomed! 'Tis Belial, the King of Sanguine!"

Morwen held back a laugh when all the zombies and the general turned around to see the dark king. He was not there, of course. When they looked back around, Alan and Morwen were already ten feet away from them, heading straight towards town. The general roared like a hoarse bear and galloped after them, his undead troops and spirits following close behind.

Finally, Morwen and Alan reached the locked gates of Terra's Hollow and pounded on the thick wood. They shouted for someone to open up.

The undead army was only twenty feet away when a sleepy-eyed old man slid open a peep hole in the fortifications. "Hellooo, young people. What is your business heeeeere?"

Alan quickly responded, "Please, open the gates!"

"Whyyyy should I?"

Morwen looked and saw that the zombies were now ten feet away. "Please, open the gates. Quickly!"

"Whhhhhyyyyyy?"

"Alan, they're here." Morwen started to draw her sword, but she balked when she remembered that the old man was watching. Still very sleepy, the old man managed to bring his eyes up to see the army of corpses behind Morwen and Alan. His eyes widened, and he perked up.

Shut the peep hole, he shouted, "Oh, terribly sorry. I'll open it for you two."

It was too late. The zombie general grabbed Alan by his cloak collar and scooped him up high off the ground. The zombies ignored Morwen, who was frozen in shock by the gates, and they swiped at Alan from below.

His trousers tore from the touch of their long, sharp nails. The specters flew around his head, blowing their foul breath onto his face.

At last, the gates rumbled open. All of the undead army and its leader collapsed into piles of dirt. Alan fell to the ground in his badly ripped pants and black cloak.

Morwen helped him up. "Are you alright?"

"I may have scratches all over my legs, but I'm sure I'll be fine."

"Let's get you inside and to an inn. We both definitely need our rest after what happened tonight."

"Rest," Alan said, smiling, "Would be wonderful." Morwen took Alan's hand and helped him walk into the dark main street of the old, rustic town.

Chapter 11

Morwen plopped onto the bed. Alan was sprawled atop a second bed to her left, and a small nightstand and a candlestick separated them. All of their gear was piled carelessly in a corner of the inn's cramped room. Morwen brushed her hair with her comb while she watched Alan from the corner of her eye.

"Alan?" she asked.

"Yes?"

"Why do we have to stay in the same room? I would have preferred we were separate."

"Terra's Hollow is rife with thieves and outlaws. We need strength in numbers if the inn is raided or our room's lock is picked."

"But I told you that I can handle myself."

"Can you handle twelve outlaws armed with clubs and crossbows?"

Thanks to the Brand, Morwen was nearly invincible, but she kept that fact to herself. "Maybe," Morwen said.

Alan sat up and untied his braid, allowing his thick, bronze hair to ripple past his shoulders. He glanced at Morwen. She got up to return the brush to her satchel, almost tripping over her own feet. She dug through her bag. Armando had packed a few of his smaller shirts—which were still entirely too big for her—and a pair of shoes. She sighed.

"What's wrong?" Alan asked.

"I think I'll have to sleep in my filthy clothes from now on."

Alan grinned. "You say you're fearless in the face of danger, but you cringe at this?"

"It would be inconsiderate of me to get dirt all over the blankets."

"You'll be fine. The brownies come out in the mornings to clean all the rooms, anyway."

"I know about brownies," she told him. "An entire clan of them used to live in my village and eat all the filth in our homes. Oh, I remember how I listened to their high-pitched giggles at sunrise. It was magical. But when I was nine elf years old, the elders expelled the little things because they thought the brownies' help would 'make us lazy.'"

"That's horrible. That's why I appreciate that I was raised by my parents in the woods. I think adventurous elves like you and me should not be stuck in a strict little town."

"I agree. I would go insane if I traveled with someone who lectured me on elven culture every day."

"I probably would, also," he said, yawning. "If you don't mind, I'm going to sleep now. It is already very late."

Alan sat up, slipped off his cloak, and tossed it onto the floor. He pulled off his shirt and kicked off his leather boots. They hit the wall and stuck dirt and moss on the aged wood.

Morwen's cheeks grew very hot. Alan had an incredibly muscular upper body. Though she still didn't consider a friend yet, she could admit that he *was* good-looking. She shook her head to break the spell, and she asked, "May I see the map? I . . . want to see how far we are away from Kain's castle."

His hair rippled when he nodded. "Believe me, Morwen, we are anywhere but close."

"But I still want to see before I sleep."

Alan reached into the right pocket of his torn pants and pulled out an empty hand. His hand dove into his other pocket, but the map wasn't there, either. His concerned eyes met Morwen's. "Where is the map?"

"You should know. You were carrying it," Morwen said. She jumped off her bed and into the corner, rummaging through all of their bags in search of the precious paper.

"Is it there?"

"No."

Alan thought for a moment, then groaned. "It must have fallen out when the corpse army attacked me. I'm sure the wind would have carried it away by now."

"What will we do, now?" Morwen slumped back onto her bed. "If we don't have the map, we will never make it there in time!"

"We can hire ourselves a scout. The people here have memorized every square inch of this country, so we don't need a map anymore. The problem is solved, so how about we calm down and get some sleep?"

"Well, *goodnight*," Morwen said grimly, none too happy with this new circumstance. She jerked the covers up to her neck and closed her eyes. It felt awkward to have someone else in the room with her.

"Goodnight, dear."

Morwen's eyes flew open. "Dear?"

Alan chuckled. He blew out the candle on the nightstand and retreated into his covers. He rolled over, facing away from Morwen, and fell silent.

Morwen frowned. *Dear. Huh.* Before she could ponder his nonsense any more, she fell into a deep sleep.

Morwen welcomed the morning and the warm sunlight that spilled into the room from the nearby dusty window. A faint giggle came from beneath her bed. Her and Alan's bags shifted for a moment, and suddenly all the dirt and grime on them vanished.

"Brownies," Morwen whispered. The pattering of small feet on the wooden floor joined the high-pitched laughing. Morwen smiled when little shadows blocked the sun's rays and disappeared. The brownies' presence transformed the worn room into a magical realm of play. *Crunching* noises came from Alan's side of the room. She looked to her left, but Alan still slept soundly, lightly snoring. *How could he be missing this?*

Morwen slid out of bed and slipped on her glove. She tiptoed towards the other side of the room. The mud and moss on the wall by Alan's boots shrank into nothingness. She kneeled down and touched the area where the filth used to be, and hundreds of quiet squeals tickled her ears.

"Oh, I'm sorry," Morwen said.

The feet scrambled past her, and the little voices fell silent. The room lost its magic instantly.

Alan stirred under his covers. Morwen looked up and saw him still in bed, but a strange person in a black robe was leaning over him. The person's long, bright crimson hair spilled onto the sheets.

He turned towards Morwen and grinned at her with a flicker of his ominous yellow eyes.

"Ah, good morning, Morwen. It seems like you are doing well."

Morwen leaped to her feet. "Not when *you* are here."

Tobias shook his head and waved his finger at her. "Always so impolite to company. You should be ashamed of yourself."

"What do you want?" Morwen asked through her teeth.

"Have we not been through this before?" Tobias groaned as he approached her. He snatched her right wrist and held it up to his face. He pulled off the glove. "I believe *you* are what I came for, Morwen, and I plan to leave with you, also."

"No you won't. I can stop you. I have help," she said, nodding her head at Alan. She tried to wrench her wrist from Tobias's hand.

"Oh, are you so sure about that?"

Tobias held his free hand out to his side as if he was introducing a stage performance. He let go of Morwen's hand and stepped aside. Alan disappeared in a flash. A gigantic being, covered in light brown fur, soared towards Morwen, pinning her to the wall with its large paws.

"W—W—Werewolf!"

"*Wooooin*," the creature howled in her face. "*Wooorwen* . . . *Worrrrrwen* . . . *Mooooorwen* . . . Morwwwen . . . . "

Morwen blinked and saw Alan frantically shaking her by the shoulders. She cocked her head to the side and looked at him, confused.

The werewolf was gone.

"Morwen, you were in a nightmare. You're safe."

"No, he might still be here."

"Who?"

"*Nobody*," she said quickly, pushing Alan away.

He opened his mouth to speak, but then shut it quickly. He turned around and picked up his shirt and cloak and put them on. He stepped into his boots. "Quickly, Morwen. Let's pack up and go look for a scout to hire."

"Right now? But what about breakfast? We need our strength to travel."

"You can eat at the pub downstairs while *I* go hire a scout."

"Won't you eat?" Morwen asked as she followed him to the door.

"Could you snatch me a biscuit?" He pulled his bag over his back, fastened all his weapons, and started to take Morwen's sword.

She grabbed it. "*I* can handle that, thank you."

"Just trying to be a gentleman," he growled. He hurried into the hallway and went down the staircase to the first floor.

The bedroom door eased shut, and Morwen went over to her satchel and pulled her glove over her scaly hand. She put on her beaded slippers and slid her satchel onto her back. As she headed out of the room, she looked back, thinking about the nightmare.

She shivered and headed into the hallway. On its wall hung framed lists of Emperor Artaxiad's laws. She hurried past. Dressed as a warrior and carrying a sword with her, she broke the law. She and Alan had to leave town before anyone reported her.

Morwen reached the pub on the ground floor of the inn and found a small table by a window. She sat down and set her bag by her feet. She searched around her sack and found the pouch of gold coins Armando had slipped inside. She walked over to the innkeeper at the bar's counter and politely asked for a loaf of bread.

"Young lass, yeh've got quite an appetite this mornin'!"

"I'm buying for a friend, also."

"Now I see! That'll be six gold pieces, if yeh please."

Morwen plucked six coins from her bag and dropped them into the innkeeper's meaty hand.

"Thank yeh very much. I'll tell the cook just wha' yeh need and he'll bring a loaf out. He's made a fresh batch about an hour ago."

"Thank you."

Morwen returned to her table and sat in its craggy wooden chair, staring blankly out the window. She perked up when she saw Alan striding up a lane between two rows of pale, dusty buildings. He entered a dark tavern and shut the door behind him. Morwen remembered her dream again and shook from the chill on her neck. *Alan, a werewolf? Ridiculous.*

She went over the events again as the inn's cook set her breakfast in front of her. He was a cheery, middle-aged man—much like the innkeeper—with a moustache big enough to use as a wig. His tall, pointed ears wiggled when he smiled.

She grinned back at him. "Thank you, sir."

"Such *fine* manners, young lady. Yer welcome."

The cook hurried back into the kitchen as Morwen looked at her breakfast. She slowly picked off and ate pieces of the loaf. No matter how much she tried to rid her mind of it, the dream kept repeating itself in her head. *Of course it was just a dream. But why didn't Alan come when I asked him to help me out? . . . Because he wasn't there. In the dream. Or maybe he didn't come because he was . . . no, he couldn't have been that werewolf. Impossible!*

At least, Morwen *hoped* it was.

As Morwen finished eating her half of the bread, she looked up and—to her surprise—saw Alan standing next to her with a boy at his side. The boy's ears were not pointed, nor were his cheekbones very high at all. He was obviously a human. A black cloth mask hid his face from the nose down, and he was dressed modestly in baggy bull-hide pants, a dirty peach-colored blouse—similar to Alan's—and a lightly armored vest. He wore beautiful knee-high boots that were heavily beaded from below his knee down to his ankle. His eyes were unusually soft and feminine, and his straight, rich brown hair fell down to his small shoulders. Morwen guessed him to be about seventeen in human years.

"Hello, Morwen, meet our scout for the trip," Alan said.

"Pleased to meet you."

The boy didn't respond.

"Alan, is he deaf?"

"No. I'll explain about him when we leave town."

Suddenly, the door to the inn crashed open, startling the bar patrons nearby. A tall, sturdy, blonde man, too large and bulky to be quite human, half-stumbled into the inn. He wielded a massive battle axe in his paw-like hands.

His face was red with fury, and he snorted angrily, his icy blue eyes shifting like a cat's. He spotted Alan and pointed at him with a thick finger. His axe wobbled threateningly. "I've got yeh—yeh f—f—filthy Mindite. You shall—you shall," he said, hiccupping, "Die by my hand. F—Filthy . . . ."

Morwen stood up and glanced at Alan. "Who is he talking to?"

"Me, apparently. He's completely drunk."

"This early in the morning?"

"Judging by his fair features and bulk, he's from the far south—in the frozen wasteland, Arkarskarinn. He must've had a few too many meads last night."

"Then who are Mindites?"

The Ark man lumbered up to them. "You—you. You filthy beasts—beasts, filthy Mindites from the west."

Alan whispered, "Mindites are from Mindor, Arkarskarinn's neighbor. They've been feuding for the past century. They resemble elves."

The man held his axe high above his head. The heavy weapon was too cumbersome for his intoxicated muscles, though. He wobbled on his feet and dropped his battleaxe onto a nearby chair. The worn wood split in two.

Alan looked the Ark straight in the eye and said, "I'm sorry, but I think you have us mistaken for someone else."

"Yer—Yer dark hair. Yer hair. It's dark. That means yer a Mind—*hic*—Mindite."

"We are not that bulky like Mindites at all."

The Ark man swayed on his feet and almost fell over. "But yer dark hair."

Morwen quickly tossed the bread into her bag. She leaned over to Alan and whispered, "He's too drunk to listen. On my signal, we run out of town."

Alan nodded while she grabbed the bag.

Morwen counted with a whisper, "One, two . . . go!" She sprinted around the man, and Alan grabbed the scout's wrist, pulling him along.

The trio dashed towards the door as the Ark roared in anger and chased shakily after them. Morwen swung the door open and dashed outside, with Alan and the scout following close behind. The Ark man was already gaining on them with his unnaturally heavy strides, but the trio was almost to Terra's Hollow's gates.

The commotion caused the villagers around them to stop what they were doing and gawk. The trio stormed out gates and kept on sprinting until they came to a forest—separate from the Silvia Forest—outside of the town, at the edge of the cursed field. They all three dove into a large bush and hid.

"Ouch, why a *thorn* bush?" Morwen asked.

Alan ignored her and put a finger to his lips, nodding toward the Ark, who was trudging towards them. He walked right up to their bush stared at it for a few minutes. Alan shifted his weight a little, and the entire shrub shook. Their pursuer sprang to life. His eyes grew bloodshot and angry once again.

"Sorry," Alan said.

The man clawed through the bush in an effort to catch them.

The trio clambered to their feet and darted into the forest. They came upon a large oak tree and climbed it, hiding in its strong branches and thick clumps of leaves.

They heard the thundering footsteps of the Ark man coming closer again. When he was directly below them, he stomped around the tree's roots, fiercely kicking bushes and stumps. A minute later, he sat down wearily, slumped backward, and fell asleep. Bits of grass flew into his nostrils when he snored.

Morwen sighed in relief and looked over at the unusually calm scout, who was in the process of removing his mask. Morwen's jaw dropped as she gaped at his revealed face. "You're a—a *girl?*"

Chapter 12

"Morwen," Alan said calmly. "This is Gwendolyn Corcoran, the scout for our journey."

"You hired a *female* scout? How? The laws . . . ."

"To tell you the truth, Gwendolyn and I have known each other since we were young. When I was around thirteen elf years old, my dad would take me to town whenever he needed to trade animal skins for money or other goods.

One day, I was talking with a group of boys when an adventurous three-year-old girl tottered up to us and wanted to join. Her spirit at that young age was quite funny, and I always spoke to her when Father and I visited from then on. I haven't seen her for a long time. Apparently, she's been a scout all these years and dresses as a boy to stay in her job."

Morwen eyed the girl. "Oh, so *that's* why you wore that mask over your face."

"Yes, and I'm glad that blasted thing's off," Gwendolyn said.

Though Morwen knew the newcomer and Alan were simply friends, she could not help but feel a little jealous. However, Gwendolyn seemed likable enough, and they did need a scout.

Gwendolyn shifted on her tree limb and asked, "So where are you going?"

"The castle belonging to the wizard Kain, on Mt. Schism," Morwen answered.

Gwendolyn's eyebrows rose, and she whistled in awe. "That's quite a ways. It'll probably take a good month or so to get there. Why do you want to go *there*?"

"Long story short," Morwen said. "I have a . . . a mental disease, and the only person who can remove it—I mean—heal me, is Kain."

"Oh really," Gwendolyn said, as she climbed down. "If you're the kind of loon who talks to herself at night, I'll make sure I sleep in a separate camp each night."

"I don't talk to myself!"

"Then what do you do? Have fits? Insist you can fly from the tops of towers?"

"No," Morwen said, getting a little annoyed. "I just have some problems that can be overwhelming for me—at times."

"Overwhelming," Gwendolyn echoed, frowning. "Well, just so you know, I'm very capable of holding you off if you try to kill me or something."

"I'm more dangerous than you think. Maybe I'll tell you more, later. We need to get going."

"Fine, then," Gwendolyn said. "Call me *Lyn*, for short."

Alan and Morwen climbed down the tree and came to her side. The trio hiked briskly through the woods, with Lyn leading the way. A few hours later, Lyn stopped short in front of grove of weeping willows.

"What's wrong?" Alan asked.

"Hush."

Lyn tiptoed into the sea-green cascades and pushed them slightly aside, revealing a camp of five large, rugged tents surrounding a freshly doused fire.

Lyn muttered, "It's a thief camp."

Morwen leaned over to Lyn and whispered, "How about we go around it? If we get caught, it'll only waste time."

Alan poked his face between theirs. "But what if they have scouts out in the woods? If they see us when our backs are turned, they could ambush us from behind. We should attack them while we can."

"Attack them?" Morwen countered. "Are you insane?"

Lyn held up her hands for silence. "Let's see if we can evade them. But be ready to fight just in case."

Morwen touched the hilt of her sheathed sword.

"Alright, everyone. Let's go—*carefully*," Lyn said. She made her way through the thick bushes and light willow branches with Alan and Morwen close behind.

"Lyn," Alan asked with a loud whisper. "Do you think there will be any—"

"Traaaapps!" Morwen shrieked as she was wrenched off the ground by her ankle. A rope had snatched her upwards, and she dangled upside down from a tree limb.

The bushes nearby started to rustle, and Alan and Lyn braced themselves below Morwen, standing back-to-back. Lyn pulled throwing stars—brand-new technology from a blacksmith in Terra's Hollow—out of her pocket, and Alan readied his bow.

Suddenly, Morwen heard several whistling noises. Lyn let out a small moan and collapsed. Morwen craned her neck around and saw three sharp objects sticking into Lyn's neck: tranquilizing darts. Morwen started waving her hands. "Alan, watch out, they're behind you!"

The whistling noises squealed again. Morwen felt three wasp stings on her neck. As her eyes drooped, she could make out the blurry figure of Alan readying his bow and arrows to fight the attackers.

He strung an arrow into his bow. "Show yourselves."

A few branches in a tree to his right shook, and he let his arrow fly directly towards them. A faint gagging noise came from the tree, and a man dressed in dark rags and a mask fell out, the arrow protruding from his throat.

"I think I have killed your friend here," Alan called. "I know more of you are around. Now, show yourselves to me."

"Sorry, but I can't do that," a voice sneered from behind him.

As Morwen blinked sleepily, she saw something crash down onto Alan's head, and he slumped to the ground.

Morwen awakened and found herself sitting cross-legged on the ground, her wrists tied behind her back to a wooden pole. She struggled to look around until she saw Alan to her right and Lyn on *his* right. Her bound friends hadn't noticed that she'd become conscious.

"I guess *your* idea was better, Alan," Morwen chuckled nervously.

Raising an eyebrow, Alan looked to her. "*Really.*"

Morwen looked to the ground. Hearing the friends' conversation, the crooks who had captured them emerged from their nearby tents. Around fourteen men stood watching her and her friends. A woman pushed her way through the crowd and stopped in front of them.

She definitely did not look like a Farrfalan woman. This tan-skinned human wore tight leather pants, a lace-edged blouse, and a bodice that showed a shameful amount of cleavage. *She must be a woman from the island of Sternus,* Morwen concluded. The female robber bent down and put her face near Alan's, smothering him in her dark hair. Her purple-nailed fingers danced through his hair and untied his braid.

"My, my," she cooed in her heavy accent, "You are so strapping and handsome. Tell me sir, of what age are you? You may fit in well with us."

Alan's face reddened each time she rolled an "r." He cleared his throat. "Does it matter what age I am? I want nothing to do with a Sterni woman. Your people are only bandits and smugglers."

A young robber interrupted, looking at the woman. "And what fine-looking bandits and smugglers they are!"

Brushing her hair over her shoulder, the woman placed her boot on Alan's chest. "Young sir, why do you not wish to join my troupe?"

"My loyalties belong to another cause."

Raising an eyebrow, the woman swept Alan's hair away from his face. Her eyes found his pointed ears. Disgusted, she backed away from him. "Ugh. You are a slow-aging elf, no? I cannot have a lackey outlive me," she said.

She turned and walked to her tent, her hips swaying seductively. "Kill them all. We do not need these children running off and crying to the guards."

The group of bandits, enchanted by their leader's striking charisma, obeyed and drew daggers and knives from their pockets, coats, and belts. Brandishing their weapons with excitement, they prepared for the thrill of killing the human scout and pair of elves.

A blinding flash lit the forest around them, and a muffled rumble rolled through the sky.

The robbers balked and looked to the sick purple of the darkening heavens. For a few seconds, the world fell silent. In moments, a torrent of cold rain plummeted from the sky, instantly soaking everything in the area. The men coughed and spat and retreated to their tents as the clouds brought forth another thunderclap.

Lyn looked to Alan and shouted through the rain, "What a lovely mess we're in, Alan. I appreciate you leading us to our deaths!"

Morwen leaned over and yelled, "He tried his best to help. But we're not going to die. I have a plan."

Alan threw Morwen a sidelong glance and grinned, his long bronze hair sticking to his skin.

"My arm," Morwen called through the storm. "My arm can help us."

"Cut us free with your claws before the bandits see."

Lyn cocked her head. "Claws? What do you mean?"

Alan waved his hand. "We'll explain later."

Morwen, despite the tight ropes, slowly eased off her glove. Pushing a razor-sharp claw between the ropes, she jerked her hand, snapping the twine binding her. After stretching her wrists a few times, she crawled over to Alan to free him next. She froze when someone bellowed, "Hey, that girl's free!"

"Get 'er!" Another shouted as the robbers rushed from their tents.

"Morwen, use your arm again," Alan urged.

The Branding

"It might kill you and Lyn, too. I can't take the chance."

"We'll end up dead if you don't do anything!"

Morwen sobbed through the rain. "I'll use my arm, but I'll never do it again."

Coming to her feet, flexing her clawed fingers, she let her knuckles pop and stretch. *I hope my fake bravado helps.*

The enemies before her grinned, clutching their knives and daggers with obvious excitement, and slowly advanced on her.

Morwen hesitated before running towards them, her arm ready to strike. The men burst into laughter when she swiped at one of them. Lightning illuminated the dark sky, and the rain beat on them more heavily. The Sterni woman emerged from her tent and watched the commotion.

A husky bandit slung his arm around Morwen and held his knife to her throat. "Tryin' to be the little hero, eh? What adorable rubbish. You know you can't beat us."

He raked the knife across Morwen's throat. The troupe's roar of laughter overpowered her yelp of pain.

After much of her blood had escaped her wound, Morwen slumped forward in the bandit's grasp. Her Branded arm twitched and stung, and a strange chill crawled up her spine. Once it reached the top of her head, the stinging burst into a lightning bolt that ripped through her.

Her enchanted hand snaked up to her attacker's shoulder and dug in its claws.

The man shouted and flung Morwen to the ground, her claws leaving his thick flesh. "Get away from me, demon!"

Lady Cassade and Thorian appeared in Morwen's mind. Thorian leaned to his wife and asked, "Have you ever thought that she might *not* have a demon in her? She just may be one herself."

A strange force tugged at her gut and brought her into a dazed state. An odd, hidden anger flickered and grew inside her. Without thinking, she growled from the muddy ground, "*What* am I again?"

"You're a demon. A nasty, dirty demon!"

The power inside her pulled at her limbs, like a master pulling at a marionette. The Brand controlled her now.

She came to her feet and tilted her head with a smirk. Flexing her talons, she took slow, single steps towards the bandits. Morwen, observing all of this while trapped in her own body, went blind. Her hearing faltered, and the sounds of her surroundings dulled into whispers.

"Time to choose your execution," a familiar voice hissed.

Who is this? Am I speaking? Morwen felt her lips stretch into a crooked smile.

The robbers hooted and slapped their knees.

"Little lady, you have no chance of winning," a young man snickered. "What was wrong with your blade when you cut her, Griff? Does its poison turn victims into loons?"

Morwen regained her sight, and in a flash of lightning, found herself crouched over a fallen body, her claws planted deeply in his chest. The man's jaw quivered open, mimicking a fish drowning in air. Eyes closing slowly, he sighed, the rain filling his cold mouth.

"Who's next?" Morwen cackled through the downpour.

The troupe cowered before her.

The Sterni woman glanced at Morwen, then to her deceased henchman. Her eyes widened. "R—Run! Run, I say! Retreat! Follow me!" She took off, and the men followed her.

Alan and Lyn watched as the usually kind and well-mannered Morwen threw back her head and cackled to the heavens. Lightning lit the woods. The Brand's turquoise scales flashed brilliantly. Then she turned towards them, readying her claws for another fight as she approached.

"Stop!" Alan pleaded. "Th—This isn't you, Morwen, wake up. Please, wake up."

"Listen if you can hear us!" Lyn added.

"Fight it, Morwen! Fight it!"

A lightning strike nearby blinded Morwen, and when she blinked to regain her sight, she found only darkness around her. A cold, faint light bloomed behind her. She turned and gasped, stumbling backward. She had almost fallen over the edge of a dark crevasse. It surrounded the glow, protecting it. Morwen squinted into the light that pierced her eyes. A dazzling orb, shining with a brilliant rainbow halo, floated in silence. She watched the orb, mesmerized by its beauty, then jumped when someone spoke from behind her.

"Beautiful, isn't it?"

Morwen turned, finding a twin of herself standing nearby. Strangely, the other Morwen's hair shone a bright crimson, and her glowing, harvest moon eyes watched her carefully.

Morwen's twin smirked. "I can't wait to eat it up. It's just too lovely to resist!"

The real Morwen scowled. "Get out of my mind, Tobias!"

Her double giggled. "Blockhead, I am the Brand! And *you* are now my host. Don't worry; we'll both become the same person soon. I simply need to snatch up that *lovely* soul of yours. If you help me cross this ravine, I can reach it, but only your willpower will let me cross."

"Why would I let you have your way? I'm going to get rid of you soon, I assure you. I'll win this fight."

"Oh *really*? Then why am I controlling your body right now? It seems like *I'm* the one winning."

Morwen ignored it. "What are you doing to Lyn and Alan?"

"If you were more willing to embrace me, I'd at *least* let you see what's going on outside. Your rudeness to Master Tobias and me is insulting."

"Give me back my body. I'll fight you for it if I have to."

"Fair enough." The Brand cringed, allowing shiny, turquoise scales to race across its body. Its fingers sprouted sharp, black talons, and sharp fangs sprang from its mouth. Large, antelope-like horns grew from the top of its forehead, and a long, spike-ended tail extended from its back end, then curled at its feet.

Tucking its hair behind its ears, the Brand stood up straight. "How do you like your future body? Don't fret; you'll be able to look like this, too, shortly. If you surrender right here, I'll ensure that the change will be painless."

"I don't plan on changing at all, thanks." Morwen ran towards the Brand and pounced on it.

The Brand grabbed Morwen by the collar and flung her away with ease.

Morwen landed on her back and skidded across the smooth ground. Her mind fumbling for a plan, she jumped to her feet and charged the Brand again. The Brand's tail wrapped around her ankle, tugging Morwen off her feet, and tossed her to the nearby ravine. Morwen caught the edge with one hand, then the other.

The Brand strolled up to Morwen and smacked her face with its tail. Throwing back its head back and laughing, the Brand did not realize Morwen had grabbed its tail until the young warrior heaved it downwards. The Brand danced, unbalanced, to the edge of the crevasse and fell into the darkness.

"I am not finished yet," it shrieked. "Our fight has only begun!"

Wincing for a last burst of energy, Morwen pulled herself over the edge of the ravine and came to her feet. In a few blinks of her eye, the outside world melted into sight. Control sat in Morwen's hands once more.

Alan and Lyn, still bound on the poles, sat wide-eyed before her. Alan's face, covered with minor scratches and cuts, still managed to pull into a hopeful smile.

Lyn shook a little, her feet kicking the grass in hopes of backing away from Morwen. The rain had let up for the moment, but the dark clouds still hung heavily in the sky. Morwen shook her head and fell to her knees.

Alan's eyes brightened. "Morwen? Is this you?"

She nodded. "Oh, Alan, I'm so sorry for doing this to you! It . . . took over me. I couldn't stop it."

"Calm down, it's over now. I'll be okay and so will Lyn. All *we* have to worry about now is finding some decent shelter before another storm comes."

Morwen nodded and cut Alan and Lyn free. Lyn stood and shook her head, calming her nerves, while Alan searched the bandits' tents. Alan peeked out from behind a tarp. "I've found our gear."

The three of them retrieved their bags and weapons and left the area quickly.

"As I said before, we should find shelter before another storm hits. I don't want anyone falling ill," Alan said.

Morwen and Lyn both nodded as they looked up the ever-darkening sky.

Lyn added, "I know there's a lake in this area, and it's completely surrounded by caves, so maybe we should look there. If you can see that large hill through the trees a ways northwest from here—yes, look a bit your right—the lake's just on the other side of it."

"Excellent. Let's go."

Morwen, Alan, and Lyn darted off in the direction of the hill while the sky rumbled ominously. The air around them turned even colder, and the wind chased them through the maze of trees. As the three friends ran faster, the wind grew more frigid and howled in protest.

"Alan, we won't make it," Morwen called through the gale.

"Yes, we can. Run faster!"

The team struggled to reach the hill through the overpowering gusts. Right as they reached the foot of the hill, a startling flash of lightning welcomed a downpour of rain. Thunder crashed around them. Lyn and Alan scaled the hill, slippery with fresh mud, with great ease, but inexperienced Morwen kept losing her footing and sliding down the hill. Lyn laughed until she fell over backwards, but Alan hurried to give Morwen a helping hand.

Once he tugged her to the top of the hill, Morwen asked, wiping the mud off her pants, "Where are the caves?"

Lyn moved to the other side of the hill, where the trees opened up to reveal a valley with a lake at its center. Small caves dotted the area, giving Morwen, Alan, and Lyn a good chance of finding shelter through the storm.

"Hurry," Lyn said. She stepped carefully down the hill, occasionally slipping on the wet grass. Morwen and Alan followed her, and they eventually came upon a large, damp cave.

Morwen balked before entering. "Do you know if anything *lives* in there?"

"No," Alan said. "Even so, I'd risk it to get out of this freezing rain."

"I agree," Lyn said. Stepping into the cave, they threw off their bags and weapons and set them against the wall. Soaking wet and shivering, the three friends sat down near the cave's mouth.

"We need a fire, now, don't we?" Morwen asked. "The firewood will be soaked, though, in this rain."

"Not when you have magic," Lyn said, smiling. "I'll find some sticks."

"Magic?" Morwen said. "I thought magic was reserved for elders and wizards."

"Elves really *do* shelter their young, don't they?"

"That's why I wanted to leave my town."

"Ah. But magic devices are sold in only a few places in the world. You just need to know where to find them."

"Talk won't start a fire," Alan said. "I'll go get firewood. You two stay dry in here."

"Thanks," Lyn said.

Alan sprinted away and disappeared in the heavy rain.

Chapter 13

Once Alan was out of earshot, Morwen thought for a moment. She looked to the floor, then to Lyn. "Lyn?"

"Yes?"

"How do you, well, feel about Alan?"

"Huh? What do you mean?"

"Do you feel anything for Alan?"

"You mean, in a romantic sort of way?"

Morwen nodded.

A startling laugh—almost a cackle—burst from Lyn's mouth and echoed off the chilly cave walls. "What a *random* question," she said, still giggling a little. "I just see Alan as a good friend. Nothing more. Why do you ask?"

Morwen hesitated.

A grin stretched across Lyn's face. "Oh, you're a little smitten with him, aren't you?"

"No," Morwen said quickly.

"Yes, you are"

"Shush! He might hear us."

"You wouldn't want that now, would you?"

Unable to think of a witty response, Morwen slapped Lyn playfully on the arm, making sure to use her safe hand. Lyn glanced at the red stamp of Morwen's hand on her arm, then looked up. She shook her head, returning Morwen's slap with a friendly smile.

Morwen hesitated. "Aren't you afraid of this—problem I have?" She turned her clawed hand over to look at her palm.

"*Another* random question." Lyn tapped her temple with her finger. "Morwen, I have good instincts. You should know that by now. If I feel something bad is going to happen, I'll leave. I'll come back when I think it's safe, though, don't worry. Besides, from what I saw a while ago, Alan's support helps you keep your fits in check."

Morwen blushed and bit her lip to hold back a smile.

"When do you want your wedding date to be, Lady Saratogas?" Lyn muttered with a nudge.

Morwen's eyes widened. "Hush!"

Lyn laughed, and Morwen felt her face grow hotter. Lyn's laughing fit was contagious enough for Morwen to join in. They fell silent when a sodden figure emerged from the rain.

"Who is getting married?" Alan asked.

The two girls froze and glanced at each other.

Morwen stuttered a quick answer. "A young elven man. In my village. He is to marry a—um—very nice elven girl."

Alan, eyeing them, came into the cave carrying an armload of large twigs and sticks. He dropped them onto the ground and stretched his muscles. His long hair dripped water onto the cave floor, and he shivered slightly. Lyn drew a small stick from her pocket. The bright red cap on the twig was a substance Morwen could only guess at. Lyn swiped the stick across her leg, the red material combusting into a small tongue of fire.

"What's that?" Morwen and Alan asked.

"You elves haven't seen much of this world, have you? *This* little twig is called a 'match.' It starts a fire when you drag its red tip across a rough surface."

"Is *that* the magic you were telling us about?" Alan asked while gawking at the mystical flame.

"No, but it *is* a fairly new invention sold by some Farrfalan folks. By the way, Morwen was right that the wet sticks won't light by normal means. *This* is where the magic comes in."

Lyn held the match in front of her lips, just far enough away to not burn her, and closed her eyes. She leaned over the pile of twigs, blowing gently onto the flame.

The little flicker on the match stretched into a snake of fire that snapped its jaws at the wet timber. Lyn opened her eyes and threw the match into the pile. She watched the snake rest in a coil on the wood and light it into a warm, welcoming bonfire.

"Thanks, Lyn." Alan said, rubbing his hands together near the heat. "We'd better change out of our wet clothes, too. Dry off with this." He pulled a blanket from his pack.

"Thanks." Lyn said, suddenly smiling, "But we're not changing out here in front of you, though."

Morwen tried not to laugh as Alan's ears and cheeks burned a bright red. Shifting his weight, he looked to the ground and said, "Well, how about you two dry off in the back of the cave? I promise I won't follow you there."

"Of course you won't." Lyn smirked, rolling her eyes. After taking her extra clothes from her bag, she hurried off toward the back of the cave. Morwen followed with her own change of clothes. Surprisingly, the cave stretched quite a ways back. The girls followed the cave until they stood in nearly complete darkness.

Morwen tapped Lyn's shoulder. "Let's not go any further. It's dark; we might fall into a hole or something."

"I can use my matches to light this place," Lyn bragged as she struck a match across her pants leg. It extinguished itself the moment it lit. "Hmm." She tossed the match aside and lit another. "Bad match."

The match flared and died again by some mysterious wind, and the two girls glanced around. They dropped their things and stood back-to-back, watching for anything that might be lurking nearby.

A taut, smooth substance brushed up against Morwen's arm, and she gasped in surprise. "I don't think we're the only ones back here."

"Don't get worried yet. It's probably Alan playing a trick on us."

"I don't think he's *that* kind of person."

"You're right, b—but there's always a first time for anything, right?" After Lyn finished, she paused, then shivered. "Something just brushed up against my neck. Alan would *never* touch me that way."

"Be ready to fight, then."

All was silent until Morwen felt a faint breeze pass her ear. She threw a punch into the darkness, and her fist met soft material. A loud thump echoed throughout the cave. "Lyn, I got it. Light a match, quickly."

Morwen dropped to her knees as her victim was illuminated. A young man—definitely not in his teens—rested, unconscious, on the damp cave floor. At first glance Morwen assumed he was human, but his appearance kept getting stranger the longer she examined him.

His straight black hair fell to the middle of his neck, his skin a rich tan tone. What made his appearance so peculiar was his all-black wardrobe. He wore a long, black leather trench coat—one very similar to that of a sneaky, shadow-blending rogue—and a layer of chain mail armor on his chest underneath. His breeches and buckled shoes looked like they had been sewn for a funeral rather than for everyday wear.

Lyn crouched next to the man's head. "He looks like a criminal."

"But what if he isn't? What if he's a tired traveler who just needed shelter from the rain, like us?"

"I understand your point, but sometimes you just have to follow that feeling in your gut instead of your heart."

Morwen pursed her lips and thought for a moment. "I guess you're right. Well, based on *your* idea, what should we do with him? We're out in the middle of nowhere, and there are no jails or bounty collectors for miles around. But if we leave him alone, he'll definitely come after us again."

"That's true, so maybe we should—wait, look! He's waking up."

The man's eyes blinked open. Once he saw Lyn and Morwen standing over him, he jumped in surprise and sat up. Shaking, he bowed his head politely and said in an unfamiliar accent, "I sincerely apologize, ladies, for scaring you. I—I thought you were one of those awful bandits from that camp nearby."

Morwen watched Lyn's tough exterior melt at the sound of the man's voice—probably his bright pink eyes, too.

Pink? This man definitely isn't the average criminal. I've never heard of people with brightly-colored eyes. Is he some kind of monster, then?

"Don't worry," Morwen said. "We've taken care of them."

"Call me Liam. Liam Forbys Iassen."

"Liam," Lyn repeated, her eyes somewhat glossing over.

Morwen leaned over to Lyn and whispered loudly, "He is much too old for you."

Lyn scowled at her as Liam stood and asked innocently, "I beg your pardon?"

The girls came to their feet. Lyn forced a smile. "Nothing." Morwen hardly contained her amusement when Lyn batted her eyelashes at the man. "Ahem, *Liam*—"

"Yes?"

"I—I would like to show you our camp for the night. I'm sure it's very lonely in this cave, and you look like you need some decent food in you."

"Lyn, no," Morwen said, leaning to her ear. "What about what you just said? He could be dangerous."

"She is right," Liam said, straightening his posture. "I may be dangerous, though I know that I certainly am not. I am quite a gentleman."

"If you aren't dangerous," Morwen asked, stepping up to him. "Then do you mind if I ask you something?"

Pausing for a moment, Liam nodded.

"Are you human?"

"Of course I am."

"Then why do you have pink-colored eyes?"

"I—nearly went blind from an injury as a young boy. Much of the blood that rushed to my eyes is still there. I—I do not like talking about it."

"That's terrible," Lyn said.

Morwen was adamant. "Blood is red, is it not? Why pink? Why can't you keep your stories straight? Are you a criminal?"

"Morwen!" Lyn protested.

Liam furrowed his eyebrows and said slowly, "I surely am not a criminal. I am a scholar, and I know that when blood pools in eyes it most certainly turns the irises pink!"

"Irises?"

"Now *that* proves I am a scholar, and you are not. Now please, rid yourself of your hostile attitude. You may make rash decisions because of it."

"Just being smarter than someone does not give you the title of scholar, but I know someone trained honorably in a weapon is a warrior. And *I* am a warrior," Morwen said. Her clawed hand touched her lips in surprise after she spoke. She had not said something so confident in quite a while.

Lyn gave Morwen a pleading look. *Where had the strong, confident Lyn gone?*

Morwen finally gave in to her friend's stare. "Because of Lyn's urging, I'll let you stay with us, but if you start acting even a little strangely, I shall make sure you don't bother us again."

"Please, come and eat with us!" Lyn said as she took Liam's hand, tugging him to the mouth of the cave.

Morwen picked up the dropped clothing and blanket, and she followed cautiously, still wary about this "Liam." At last Lyn, Morwen, and Liam reached the crackling fire. The storm still beat upon the cave from outside.

Alan threw Liam an extremely bewildered—almost hostile—look. "Where did *he* come from?"

"We found him in the back of the cave, and *I* invited him to dinner," Lyn said proudly as she sat down next to the flames. She pulled Liam down, too.

Morwen rolled her eyes and dropped the extra clothing onto the floor. She joined Alan by the fire.

"I gathered tree nuts and berries while you two were gone. Here, eat." Alan clutched a large sack next to him. He unloaded a small pile of the food into his lap and tossed the bag to Morwen, who took some, also. She passed it to Lyn and Liam. Lyn pulled a few handfuls of nuts and berries from the sack, then shoved the rough bag into Liam's hand. Morwen, already eating her dinner, gave Alan a confused look while nodding towards her friend.

Leaning over to her, Alan muttered, "That's just how Lyn deals with men she's, well, *completely mad* about. Trust me, when I started talking to her more often, she did the same to me, and I eventually had to go hide in an empty rum barrel to escape her clutches."

Morwen laughed and continued to eat.

Liam, on the other hand, refused to consume anything at all, despite Lyn trying to coax him into doing so. As he politely struggled to push Lyn away, his pink eyes looked to Morwen. He watched her for a second, and he asked, "Pardon my staring, young lady—"

"Please call me Morwen."

"*Morwen*, why are you covered in blood? Are you wounded?"

Choking on food after she gasped in surprise, Morwen looked down at herself, her neck and clothing splattered with blood—she still hadn't changed her clothes.

"Well, I—" she said, trying to think quickly.

Liam's eyes lowered to stare at Morwen's turquoise-scaled hand and black claws. "And what is wrong with your hand?"

Trying to think of how to tell of her plight, Morwen sighed. Her problem literally grew worse every day—and even harder to hide.

"Well, Liam, I have this... *curse* on me, and it spreads across my body like a rash. It makes me go into mad fits, too, and if the curse envelops my whole body, I'll—die. But the curse does give me special powers while I live. I am almost completely invincible. So, when my throat was slit earlier this afternoon, nothing *too* terrible happened. I'm traveling with Alan and Lyn to find a man who can take the curse away."

"Where is the place you are traveling to?"

"Mt. Schism," Morwen said slowly, warily. She was telling this stranger a great deal about her circumstances. "We need to find a wizard. A master wizard. We need to get to his castle as soon as possible."

"But as *everyone* knows," Lyn added matter-of-factly. "Mt. Schism is in the dead center of a tall, rocky, and treacherous mountain range. So the journey will take us a while. Hopefully, we'll make it in time."

"Oh! Oh!" Liam exclaimed. "I know a shortcut there."

Everyone around the fire fell silent, and Morwen's jaw dropped so low that her spittle started to drip down her jaw. Then Alan set down his flask of water.

"You *do*?" Morwen asked, wiping her mouth to get serious again. "But you know what I said. If Lyn suspects that you're misleading us, expect to be dealt with swiftly, right Lyn?"

Lyn nodded while gazing at Liam. She sighed deeply.

Liam glanced at Morwen and asked, "Do you still not trust me enough when I have not attacked you while you were eating and your weapons were set aside?"

"You bothered us in the back of the cave. So I still can't decide about you. What do *you* think, Alan?"

"I can't decide, either, but I support your plan for dealing with him if he causes trouble. He very well might have useful information for us."

"Welcome to our group, then," Lyn said.

"Thank you. I promise I shall bring you to Mt. Schism in the fastest way possible. You have my word."

Morwen threw the rest of her dinner into her mouth, then took a sip from the water flask by Alan. She yawned and stretched her arms outward. "We'll head out tomorrow, then. I don't know about you three, but I'm exhausted. I'm going to bed after I clean up."

Lyn also yawned, then Alan grunted and stretched his arms. After grabbing a blanket to dry off, Morwen headed into the back of the cave.

"Let's roll out the mats," Alan said. He and Lyn took out three thick wool blankets, each long enough to wrap up a person into a baby-like bundle. Turning to Liam, he said, rather insincerely, "I'm sorry we don't have enough bedrolls for you."

"Do not worry; I do not need sleep much anyways. I can keep watch."

"That's so kind of you," Lyn said, not noticing Morwen returning and dropping a bloodstained blanket nearby. Alan threw Liam a suspicious glare.

"I won't do anything bad, Alan. So please, rest easy."

Morwen, Alan, and Lyn soon sprawled out on their mats and pulled the soft edges of their blankets up to their necks. Liam, instead, sat staring at the fire, hugging his knees. The rain still danced on the roof of the cave.

"Goodnight everyone," Morwen said, resting her head. The others returned the goodnight. In a matter of minutes, everyone had fallen asleep except Liam.

"Oh, how boring insomnia can be," he said loudly.

Morwen opened her eyes slowly, startled by a bright light. Looking around, she found herself standing in a gorgeous green field—dotted with clumps of wildflowers—that stretched into forever. The blinding blue sky proudly held the unobstructed sun.

"Morwen," Alan called from behind her.

She turned and spotted the young elf, his hair free and flying in the wind like a river of molten copper. Smiling, he held his arms wide, awaiting an embrace. Feeling her heart swell to the point of bursting, Morwen dashed towards him and threw herself into his arms. She hugged him tightly, allowing her heart to beat near his.

"Morwen, I need something from you."

She looked up at him. "What?"

"I need . . ."

"What is it?"

The air grew cold, and Morwen brought herself closer to Alan's warm chest. All life in the field shriveled into blackness. Cracks shot across the ground. The clear blue sky vanished behind violet thunderclouds, and the wind whistled ominously past Morwen's ears.

"Alan, I'm scared! Please, tell me what you need!"

"I . . . need . . . I—I need . . . h—h—heeeeellllllpppppp!" Alan's face, now a pained grimace, looked to the sky as the wind slapped his hair onto his skin. The warm bronze locks shrouded his entire body, his chest rising and falling more quickly with each second.

Frightened, Morwen tried to escape his embrace, but Alan clutched her with shaking hands, his fingers digging into her back—she couldn't help but to yelp in pain.

Morwen tried pushing away from him with all her might. But as she struggled to escape, she felt his muscles on his lower stomach twist and grow two times its normal size. It solidified into diamond-hard flesh. His tousled hair melted onto his skin, and millions of rough, doglike hairs sprouted all over him. He grabbed Morwen by the shoulders and shoved her away with inhuman strength.

Falling to his knees, he clutched his head and cringed. His handsome, angular face morphed into a long snout, vicious red eyes, and large ears.

Morwen gawked at Alan's change. Tears spilled from her eyes when she gawked at him, now a fully transformed werewolf.

Looking her in the eye, he croaked through a maw of teeth, "Morwen . . . help. Mmmme."

The wolf rose, standing on two feet, and lunged at Morwen, knocking her onto her back with a thud. Alan leaned over her and snorted his warm, moist breath into her face. Air flew out of Morwen's open mouth, but no scream followed. Her heart rattled in her ears as he reared his head and roared, flinging his thick, hot saliva onto her face.

"Aaaaaaaaahhh!"

Morwen awoke to see Liam kneeling over her, his mouth drooling slightly. Her head turned to see that it was still dark outside the cave. *So I was dreaming.*

Liam shut his mouth and scrambled to the cave's wall.

Morwen shook her head. "What in the *world* are you doing?"

"I—I am sorry. I saw you disturbed and upset during your rest. I—I was wondering what was going on."

"But you could have always done it at a distance. Please, don't do that *ever* again."

Liam stood up and walked towards the cave's mouth.

"Wait, I'm sorry for what I said. Please don't leave," Morwen said, surprised at her sudden concern about him leaving.

"Do not worry. I am just hungry, and I need something to eat."

"Well, I'm sure there's food left from dinner." She pointed to the bag nearby.

"No, thank you. I am very . . . *particular* about what I eat."

"Fine, suit yourself," Morwen said, lying down and closing her eyes. He left quickly. Though she did get a lot of sleep that night, the visions of Alan as a werewolf still haunted her dreams.

Could he actually be . . . ? Morwen worried each time she entered the dream. *No, of course not. This is probably just a bad chain of nightmares.*

In the morning, Liam was back, and he helped cook breakfast for everyone, though he didn't eat any of it himself. Lyn tried her best to convince him to share some of the eggs they'd found in a nearby nest, but he refused to take even a bite. Once everyone finished eating, they packed up their things and set out for another long day of travel, now led by the suspicious newcomer, Liam.

"We are to head northwest from here," he said.

Morwen pointed to the map Lyn had brought with her. "But that brings us *away* from the main path through the mountain range."

"Yes, but *my* shortcut heads through the mountains in a little-known valley. Trust me; it will halve the time traveling to his castle."

Morwen gave Alan a nervous glance. He shrugged his shoulders and grinned reassuringly, patting his bow and quiver of arrows slung across his back. Morwen turned to Lyn and said, "You know, since we have a *new* scout, you can always backtrack and go home, if you like."

"No, no, I'm fine. I really want to see this lesser-known shortcut. I'd love to add it to my own map," she said as she looked over at Liam. "Besides, I really enjoy traveling with all of you."

"Then come along, my new comrades," Liam proclaimed. "Let us travel to Mt. Schism!"

Liam marched off through the woods while Morwen, Alan, and Lyn followed. They climbed out of the gulley and set out on their quest to Kain's castle once again.

Chapter 14

During the first week of travel, the team passed through a few hamlets nestled near the foot of the mountains. The final township, a human colony balanced on the mountains' starting slopes, consisted of only ten tiny log cabins and an inn. Knowing they'd be camping outdoors after this, Morwen, Alan, Lyn, and Liam treated themselves to a night in the tiny tavern.

They rented two bedrooms; Alan and Liam bunked in one two-bed room, and Morwen and Lyn stayed in its counterpart next door.

That evening, Morwen and Lyn swapped secrets and lightly gossiped into the late hours of the night. Every once and a while, their bedside candles would flicker and create frightening shadows on the wall, but the girls laughed it off. Occasionally, Morwen and Lyn could hear the boys milling around on the other side of the wall, but the noise never truly bothered them.

Morwen smiled excitedly. "You know that Emperor Artaxiad's wife has all those maidservants, right?"

"Yes, what about them?"

"Well, I heard from the bartender here that one of them has been rooted out as a male . . . *dressed as a woman!*"

Both Morwen and Lyn gasped at the rumor.

Then they jumped, startled, when a sudden bang came from their room wall. "Will you two hush?" Alan called from the other room.

Liam's muffled voice could be heard protesting. "They were not *that* loud, Alan."

The grandfather clock in the pub downstairs chimed eleven times. Wanting a good rest before traveling the next day,

Morwen and Lyn bid each other goodnight and burrowed themselves into their beds' warm wool blankets. Lyn snored lightly soon after. Morwen stepped out of bed and blew out the candles before returning to her own bed. She shut her eyes, trying to fall asleep, but she felt not the least bit tired.

Morwen rolled onto her back and stared at the ceiling. Aging moonbeams lit the room a soft, eerie gray. Oh, how she loathed the dead of night, when the invisible Spirits and Curses of the dark would skim over the shadows.

Spirits brought peaceful fantasies of beauty and bliss, but Curses carried visions of haunting terrors. Morwen took care to cover up her ears so neither could enter her head. She wished to have a deep, dreamless sleep for once.

To pass the time before drifting into slumber, Morwen peered over the top of her covers and dared herself to imagine what a Curse looked like. Suddenly, the extinguished candle on the bedside table hopped to the left. A bag shifted on the floor. The corner broom rubbed slowly against the wall.

Morwen's heart beat faster, and she shuddered, closing her eyes tightly. The young elf knew in her head that she was safe, for though monsters may have been staying in the room that night, she probably was the scariest and most dangerous of them all.

She shifted onto her side. After a while, her breathing fell slow, even, and calm. She relaxed, smiling a little, and the blanket slipped off her ears.

Morwen found herself in the sunny, flowered pasture once again.

Alan stood in front of her, his hair flying free in the summer gale. He held his arms out wide and smiled lovingly. "Morwen.".

Morwen took a deep, shaky breath. "N—No! No. Alan, I'm sorry, but I—I just can't."

Alan's arms fell to his side. The sky blackened, and the flowers wilted and shriveled into dirt. He reached out for her again. "Morwen, I need your help! Please."

Morwen shook her head, her frustration almost choking her. "No, stop. Stop it."

Alan's eyes showed his great pain as he pleaded with her. "Why do you abandon me, Morwen? I thought you loved me."

The distressed elven girl crumbled to the ground and shut her eyes tightly. "No... no. Stop it, Alan. Stop doing this to me!"

The cold wind around her slapped her face.

Alan grunted and snorted only feet away from her. He howled and pounced on Morwen.

"Stooopppp!" Morwen shot upright in bed with a shout.

Lyn jumped awake. "*Burning Belial*, Morwen! What's wrong?"

The shocked elf could not speak through her gasps and shaking. She shook her head and tried to control herself.

"A Curse got into your skull, didn't it?"

Morwen nodded quickly.

Lyn laid a hand on her friend's shoulder. "Just relax. It was just a dream, alright?"

Morwen could finally speak coherently. "You're—you're right. Thanks."

Both girls eventually fell back to sleep.

The next morning, Morwen, Alan, Lyn, and Liam woke up early and began their long trek into the mountains.

The next week, while painfully uneventful for Lyn, Alan, and Liam, tortured Morwen to exhaustion. She could hardly stand the constant werewolf dreams of Alan. After seeing the change happen before her so many times, she began to believe he truly *was* a monster in disguise. She longed to ask him about it, but her fear of losing him stood in the way of her courage. So she stayed silent.

A few weeks later, the group found a break in the mountain woods with a large lake. Deciding to rest for the afternoon, Morwen, Alan, Lyn, and Liam sat at the shore and ate, talked, and did whatever else they wished.

"Well, I want to go swimming," Lyn said suddenly. She walked off into the woods for a moment, and then sprinted out in only her thick canvas corset and bloomers.

She leaped into the shallows with a *smack*. With a flip of her feet, she swam out farther and slipped under the water. She resurfaced and found a high sandbar to stand on. Lyn came to her feet and laughed, the water plastering her hair and undergarments to her.

She waved. "Come join me, Morwen!"

"No thank you! I don't think this lake is very—um—safe to swim in."

"You're such a coward!" Lyn shouted, shivering a little. "Ooh, I can tell fall's coming. It's cold!"

"Sorry, but I don't feel comfortable being in my underwear in front of everyone."

Lyn shook her head, rolling her eyes, and leaned backwards to fall into the chilly water. She splashed about, then turned and swam to the lake's center. Her head sank under the surface, and she disappeared. She didn't resurface in quite a while.

"Lyn," Morwen called. "This isn't funny at all. Lyn?"

A feeling in her gut told her to jump into the lake. She waited a few moments to see if it was all a joke, but nobody jumped from the water to tease her. Morwen sprinted through the shallows, then fell into a swim, feeling around for her friend in the murky lake water.

Alan stood up on the shore. "Morwen, is everything alright?"

"Lyn needs help!" she cried over her shoulder. "If I go under, you and Liam will need to come rescue me *and* Lyn."

Growing more tired by the second, Morwen spent what seemed like ages—while only seconds in reality—searching. She gasped, swallowing almost a lungful of algae-laden water, when her fingertips brushed against something smooth and stiff—like an arm. Coughing, Morwen latched onto the object and heaved it upwards. A pale, unconscious Lyn surfaced. Morwen slid Lyn onto her back and struggled to bring her ashore. Morwen continued to cough the lake water from her lungs as she dragged her friend onto the sand. Alan, Morwen, and Liam stood over Lyn.

"Somebody give her air," Morwen said. "I don't know how."

Alan opened his mouth to speak, but Liam interrupted him and said, "*I* shall save Lyn's life."

Alan scowled as his companion kneeled down, pressed his lips to Lyn's, and blew air into the girl's lungs. Lyn's eyes fluttered open, and she choked to life. Liam helped her sit up. Seeing who had saved her, Lyn swooned and nearly fell back onto the shore. Liam sat rigidly on the sand, not knowing what to do.

Lyn's eyes became glossy, fawning. "Oh, you're so *wonderful*, Liam. I owe you my life."

His pink eyes flashed for a moment. "You are welcome. Come, everyone, let us continue on our journey."

Morwen helped Lyn to their pile of belongings nearby. As her friend leaned on her shoulder for support, Morwen asked, "Liam, how could you heal Lyn so quickly? It looked almost too easy."

Liam puffed out his chest. "As I said before, I am a scholar. I know much about how the body works, like how blood flows through the veins."

Morwen sighed at his arrogance and decided not to fuel his pride any more. She could not be too angry at him. After all, he had just helped save her best friend's life. Lyn pushed off of Morwen and walked shakily to her things. Morwen, Alan, Lyn, and Liam picked up their belongings and continued their journey to Kain's castle.

During the fourth week of their journey, Morwen and Lyn spent the days chatting to each other, occasionally commenting about the orange pine needles and yellowing leaves that fell from the branches above.

Through every swell and fall of the land, Alan and Liam squabbled over every topic imaginable, especially about the decision of which direction to go.

Male bonding? Morwen wondered.

Alan balled a fist as he made a witty comeback to Liam's comment.

No, everything but.

Each time an argument melted into a near fist fight between Alan and Liam, Morwen and Lyn broke the two up—like children—and made them sit away from each other to calm down. Even though Liam tried to be as polite as he could when apologizing to his companion, Alan treated Liam like he was Belial himself.

Each night as they set up camp, Alan would pull Morwen aside and tell her of his new—and old—suspicions about their new "friend". He'd speculate about why Liam left the camp every night to eat, instead of having dinner with everyone else, and Alan questioned why Liam never wanted to sleep.

Despite Alan's ramblings, Morwen still harbored a little trust in Liam ever since he helped rescue Lyn. Alan became more frustrated every time Morwen didn't believe him, and he insisted that the polite and eloquent side of Liam was only a sham covering his real self . . .

One clear, starry evening during the journey's fifth week, the troupe set up camp by the shore of the quiet Corroso River—another place Liam knew well. He'd told everyone they now traveled in the deepest part of the mountain woods.

Their spirits stayed high at the thought at how close they were to the mountain ring's inner edge around Mt. Schism. Everyone, anxious and excited to escape the forest, performed their usual camp-pitching duties with extra zeal.

Lyn stoked the fire as Morwen searched the surrounding area for firewood.

Alan found Morwen a little ways away from the river. He approached and tapped on her shoulder. "May I carry those branches for you?"

"Why thank you." Morwen, blushing, eased her armful of sticks into Alan's possession.

He leaned up against a nearby pine tree and sighed. "Morwen, I'm going to confront Liam. Tonight. He has a look in those pink 'irises'—as he calls them—that radiates trouble."

Morwen rolled her eyes with a smile. "Fine, go ahead. I still think he's a very nice young man. I mean, if he *was* so bad, he would have killed us by now and not stayed for these past four weeks."

Alan set his foot against the tree behind him for support. He looked into her eyes with an almost pleading look. "That's what he wants you to think."

"If you're going to ask *him* so many questions, then I think *you* deserve to be asked something, too."

"What's your question?"

Morwen looked to the ground. "It's . . . . "

"What? It's what?"

"Alan . . . are you—are you *hiding* anything from the rest of us?"

"No, except perhaps the emergency supply of food—you and Lyn get such massive appetites from travel. But why do you ask?"

Morwen sighed. "I—I've been having dreams lately—*visions*, almost . . . about you, and in those dreams, y—you were a—a . . . . "

"What? I was a what?" he asked with a hint of impatience.

"You were a werewolf." She pursed her lips and avoided eye contact with him.

Alan tilted his head as he watched her fidget quietly. He smiled, setting down the firewood, and he slowly—and oh so carefully—approached Morwen and wrapped his arms around her.

She embraced him with her left arm, but only inched her Branded arm towards him, lightly touching his back with it and applying not a bit more force to him. With her head on his chest, she listened to his heartbeat, soft but strong. Staring into the dark forest, she silently remembered her recurring nightmare.

Alan rested his chin on her head. "I swear to you, I am *not* a werewolf, nor do I think I ever will be one. But there is something that I want to reveal to you that *is* true—something I've wanted to tell you for a long while."

"What?"

"Morwen, I think your beauty is unmatched by any maiden. Elf, human, or anyone else. And I—I just wanted to say that—that I lo—"

Morwen's heart swelled. "Yes?"

"I—I—I'll *love* to show you that Liam is a fraud."

Morwen laughed quietly, a little disappointed, and pulled away from the hug. She bent over to pick up the pile of sticks. Alan beat her to the task and lifted them into his arms. He hurried back to camp.

"Thank you, Alan," she muttered with a slight grin. She returned to camp, also.

When Morwen sat down next to the fire, Lyn announced that dinner was ready, and Alan and Liam hurried to join them. Lyn divided the cooked deer meat amongst Alan, Morwen, Liam, and herself, and she—to no one's surprise—gave the largest piece to Liam. As usual, he refused to eat.

Alan snatched his chance to speak. "So Liam, just why don't you eat when we give you food? Are you ungrateful?"

Liam's eyes darted about, and he said, "Being such a high scholar that I am, I often fast when I need to think."

"Odd. Then why do you always leave every night to get food when we already have some here?"

Thinking, Liam stared at the ground and then looked to his companions. He grinned smartly. "I prefer being an independent person. I do not want such beautiful creatures as Morwen and Lyn to toil by the fire for me."

"Oh, that's not a problem at all." Lyn giggled, her face flushing a bright pink. "I don't mind cooking for you. Actually, I quite enjoy it."

Alan scowled and looked away, patting his knee in thought. For the rest of the meal, Alan watched Liam closely, waiting for him to make a mistake and reveal even a sliver of his supposed "bad side." Morwen, on the other hand, thought Liam's scholarly values and customs bizarre, but she quietly respected how disciplined he was to act and live as he did. Morwen turned back to her food and ate in silence.

When everyone finished their dinner—save Liam, of course—Morwen and Lyn walked to the river bank to wash the wooden plates and utensils Alan had whittled during their travels. Alan stayed back at camp with Liam and stared into the fire.

The girls soon returned to the campsite and packed away the dishes, then pulled the sleeping mats from their pile of bags. Morwen and Lyn rolled all of them out on the ground and covered each with a wool blanket. They sat on their bedrolls when they'd finished their work and began talking to each other, whispering secrets and mumbling in one another's ear.

Alan still watched the fire's flames lick the air and cough sparks to the stars. He felt a hand rest on his shoulder.

"May I join you?" Liam asked.

"Of course not, you lying weasel."

"Why do you always say that I am a bad person? A lying man? A 'deceptive traitor?'"

"Because you *are* one. You are putting on an act in front of the girls, and you know it in your own twisted black heart."

Morwen and Lyn scolded in unison, "Alan, please stop bothering Liam."

Alan's teeth clenched. He stood up, not glancing once at Liam, and walked to his mat. He lay down and jerked the blanket up to his neck. His nostrils flared, and he glared at a passing beetle.

Liam took Alan's spot by the fire.

After a while, Morwen and Lyn grew sleepy-eyed, and long, contagious yawns often interrupted their chatter. Soon, the girls slid under their blankets and slowly fell asleep.

Alan rolled over and sighed. Still not very tired, he sat up on his mat and looked to the stars. "Maybe Morwen was right," he murmured to the heavens. "Maybe Liam *is* a good man."

Alan turned around. "Liam?"

Liam wasn't there.

"He must have left to eat," Alan said, slowly coming to his feet. He glanced down at Morwen, sleeping peacefully, her green hair spread across the ground like moss. Alan jumped when a large branch broke from a tree nearby and hit the ground with a *thump*. He snatched Lyn's hunting knife and hurried over to where he heard the strange sound.

He found a gnarled branch resting on the forest floor. The black, rotted core of the wood explained why it had fallen from its perch. Sighing in relief, Alan relaxed. A large black mass nearby moved. Alarmed, he silently watched the distant woods. He saw nothing.

Clutching the hunting knife, he turned around to return to camp. When he spotted the gentle glow of the fire, he noticed Liam sitting on the ground again. Alan walked towards him until something stopped him in his tracks.

Liam glanced in all directions around the camp, then crept over to Morwen and stroked her hair gently.

Alan, suspicious again, found a nearby bush to spy from, and he squeezed the knife even more tightly in his palm. He peeked around the shrub, his foot suddenly snapping a twig. Liam's head twitched up, and he stared in Alan's direction.

Alan held his breath and froze, praying that he wouldn't be found. Liam shook his head and went back to his business. He continued to caress Morwen's soft, green hair.

Alan watched Liam gently brush Morwen's hair away from her neck. He bent over Morwen and whispered something to her, causing her to whimper and quiver in her sleep. He opened his mouth and grew large canine teeth, each about a finger's length long.

Alan burst from the bush and pounced on Liam, knocking him away from Morwen and Lyn. He pressed the knife against Liam's throat as he dragged him from camp. He slammed the struggling traitor up against a tree trunk.

Liam grinned with a newfound maliciousness, baring his large fangs.

Alan's hand shook as he held his weapon. "What in *hell* are you doing?"

"I was just retrieving my dinner. As I said, I do not want those lovely ladies to work so hard for me."

"You were going to feed off of Morwen, worm!"

Liam winced as if he had been smacked in the face, then smirked and let his dark hair fall over his glowing pink eyes. "That hurt, Alan, but I can hurt you more, mind you. Your precious Morwen? Ah, she is the most perfect victim. Her bite wound would heal in an instant! Intelligent as she is, she would never suspect that I was feeding from her."

Alan growled and took the knife away from Liam's neck. He balled a fist and drove it into Liam's nose. Liam fell to the ground with a drunken cackle as blood oozed from his nostrils. He smirked as he came to his feet, licking the red substance from his upper lip. He struck Alan's gut, and the elf flew backwards, slamming into a tree. Breathing out heavily, Alan fell limp at the base of the tree.

Alan blinked into consciousness and shook his head. He stood up and charged at Liam. Before Alan could hit him, Liam lifted his index finger and jabbed it into his attacker's forehead. The traitor chuckled in satisfaction as Alan faded into a great gust of wind. The dead leaves nearby danced into the sky.

Liam tilted his head to the side, flipping his hair out of his face before he returned to the camp. He sat down by the sleeping girls. "Oh how I crave your sweet life force, Morwen, but I am much too full with blood to feed on you again."

He cleared his throat, paused, and then shouted, flying to his feet. "Morwen, Lyn, wake up! Alan has been kidnapped by demons!"

Morwen shot upright, alert and ready. Lyn awoke and sat next to her friend.

"He's gone?" Morwen asked, her mind now whirling with thoughts. *Where should we go? What demons took him? Tobias's demons?*

"Y—Yes, he—he has disappeared! I tried to rescue him, but they were too quick for me."

Lyn slinked over to Liam and hugged him tightly, almost pushing him to the ground. "Oh, Liam, you were so brave to try and rescue Alan!"

Morwen slid off her mat and started rolling it up. "We should try and rescue him as soon as possible."

"When? Now?" Lyn asked, watching her friend pack up.

"Yes, right now. I'll be too worried to sleep again."

Lyn smiled. "Liam can take us on the shortcut to Kain's castle as soon as possible."

Morwen nodded. "Right! Since Kain's so powerful, he probably has hundreds of subordinates waiting on his every command. They can all help us save Alan."

Lyn nodded, and they all packed up their bags, making sure all of their possessions were there. Liam carried the heaviest load—both his own and Alan's bags—to be polite. After Morwen and Lyn doused the fire, Morwen looked up at the stars. *We'll rescue you, Alan. I promise.* The trio trudged off into the dark forest, heading directly for the inner slope of the cold, rocky mountain ring.

Chapter 15

When Liam had jabbed his index finger into Alan's forehead, the world around Alan disappeared into blackness, and his stomach flipped inside him as he fell through the dark. Wind danced through his hair, gently undoing his braid.

He closed his eyes, waiting for his back to snap when he hit the ground, but to his surprise, the moment never came. When he opened his eyes again, he found himself in the glimmering entrance hall of an obsidian castle.

Torches lined the walls and lead up to a wide staircase. The flames kissed their eerie reflections on the polished stone. Exotic rugs and elaborate tapestries on the floor and walls displayed only the richest shades of red. Portraits dotted the hall, their subjects' eyes glowing in bright, blinding shades of pink, yellow, blue, and green. Alan had never seen or heard of a castle this odd.

A tall, thin man appeared at the top of the staircase, his shocking blue eyes staring down at Alan. The man's silver hair cascaded down his back, and his red robe's train dragged on the floor behind him. He snapped his fingers, summoning two exceedingly attractive, bat-winged women.

The two women, their sky blue skin peeking out from their sheer, white dresses, strutted up to Alan and grabbed his arms.

"Ladies, please take Alan to the dungeon," the man said in a familiar accent.

"How do you know my name? And you sound like a young man I know."

"Be gone."

The two women took Alan down a long tunnel leading deeply into the ground—the dungeons. They dragged him into a large cell and chained him to the far wall.

Once he was restrained, he shook his head and asked, "What are you going to do to me? Please, tell me."

They shook their heads in unison and left.

The next hour Alan spent in the cell seemed to drag its feet to test his sanity. He wished out loud that something—anything—would happen, and he apparently got what he wanted.

The silver-haired man entered Alan's cell followed by a squat, unshaven man. His frighteningly large muscles squeezed at his tight, patched jacket, and his black stump of a ponytail, caked with grime and oil, made Alan cringe.

"This is him, Lucas, just as Liam had described." The silver-haired man said, pointing at Alan with a smooth, white finger. "Do with him what you wish. I do not care. Please refrain from killing him, though."

"Yes, Master," Lucas grunted. He kneeled in reverence as his superior left the room. When the heavy cell door slammed shut, Lucas arose and trudged up to Alan.

"Who are you?" Alan asked as he tugged at the chains around his wrists and ankles.

"My name's Lucas. Lucas Garouf."

"What do you want from me? If you have come to rob me, you might as well give up. I have nothing of value."

"I don't want to take yer money, boy!"

"Then what *do* you want?"

His eyes flashed yellow. "I'm hungry."

Lucas bent over slowly and hugged his chest. His hair grew so long that it touched the floor and burst from the twine holding it. His hair engulfed him and melted onto his body. He traded his skin and clothing for short, black fur and muscles that were even larger than before. The man sprouted a long snout, pointed ears, strong paws, and a bushy tail.

Alan, sweating and pressing back against the wall, glanced up at the sky outside. The moon was not full, but would be in only a few days. He trembled before this beast as its breathing became shallow.

"You should see your face right now. Horror and confusion skipping hand-in-hand." Lucas bellowed in a new, raucous voice. "Since you are so *interested* to know, I'm a Gray Werewolf, one of only a few thousand. My kind's been infected with lycanthropy for so long that we are able to transform whenever we like. Nice, ain't it?"

"You're going to bite me, aren't you? Turn me into a werewolf?" Alan did not wait for an answer. He shut his eyes tightly, but a bite never penetrated him. He opened his eyes and found Lucas's snout in his face.

Lucas growled from deep in his chest, and Alan's hair nearly stood on end. Lucas roared in amusement.

Alan began to quiver even more and swallowed hard, his eyes widening.

Lucas raised his head, revealing a maw of inch-long fangs, and sank his mouth of daggers into Alan's left shoulder.

Alan cried out as his nerves squirmed and throbbed under his skin. "Morwen," he muttered, sweat squeezing from his brow. "I'm so . . . so sorry."

Alan winced, tears stinging at his eyes for release, and watched the Gray Werewolf's purple saliva seep into his bleeding wound. Alan's infected flesh turned a contaminated maroon. Lucas slowly eased his teeth out of the muscle, leaving Alan's shoulder to visibly throb and twitch from the bite. Once Lucas took a step back from Alan, the wound numbed suddenly and grew a thick, oozing scab.

Fatigue and drowsiness overcame the young elf, and his entire body went limp, his eyes rolling back into his head. The groan of changing flesh floated to Alan's ears. The slam of the cell door followed. Alan, now a forgotten marionette on the dungeon wall, fell unconscious.

Alan awakened the next morning to find one of the blue skinned, bat-winged women standing in the corner of his cell.

She held a silver platter in her tiny hands. When she noticed that he was awake, she slinked over to him and held a clay dish and flask of water out in front of him. On the plate rested a strip of raw meat with a note pinned to it that read: "Happy breakfast, boy. If you don't like it, I don't care. Be a man and eat. This'll soon be what you'll have *all* the time. Might as well start likin' it now. –Lucas"

Disgusted, Alan shook his head at the meat. "No thanks."

"Eat," the woman demanded, her deep monotone a little unnerving.

"I'm sorry, but I can't eat this."

The woman frowned and dropped the platter to the floor with a *clang*. She picked up the flask and held it in his face. "Drink?"

"What's in there? Water?"

She stuffed the end of the flask in his mouth and tipped it upward as if she was feeding a baby. Thankfully, the drink *was* water, but it held a delicate sweetness that somehow restored his lost energy. Alan's eyes lit up, and he gratefully gulped down more. When he finished the relieving tonic, she took the flask out of his mouth. Alan licked his lips to get rid of the drool hanging off of them.

"It's sacred spring water," she said. "Water that the Master cannot drink."

"Is your master that silver-haired man from last night? Why can't he drink the water?"

The woman froze and her brown eyes widened. She cringed and covered her ears with her hands, shrieking, "I am sorry! I am sorry! I am sorry!"

She hastily piled the plate of meat and the empty flask onto the platter. Scooping it up into her arms, she screeched her apologies—to whom Alan did not know—while she retreated from Alan's cell. Her cries flew banshee-like through the dungeon hallway and became fainter and fainter until the area fell silent again.

The day passed, and Alan kept himself from going mad by watching a snail drag itself up the cell's barred windowsill, plummet to the ground, then climb back up again.

The next morning, after a night of great pain from his swelling fuchsia wound, Alan eagerly waited for breakfast, but nobody came. His stomach twisted hungrily as he hung there in the lonely cell, and after he waited until the sun was high in the sky, he assumed that the blue skinned woman was never returning.

He glared at the cell door. "He wants to starve me until the next full moon. And toss me out to hunt when I change." He fumed for the rest of the day.

For the next twenty-four hours, Alan's stomach ached more and more, and his head spun from his lack of food. His parched mouth and throat dearly missed water, and he longed for just a drop of any liquid to quench his cravings. Soon he developed laughing fits, laughing himself breathless until night fell, when he passed out from exhaustion.

The next morning—Alan's fourth day in the cell—Alan was in terrible shape. His left shoulder twitched from the frequent stinging as he hung—almost lifeless—from the stone wall. When the morning sun bloomed and lit up his cell, Alan fixated his eyes on the door. He hoped that somebody—anybody—would at least stop in to acknowledge that he was there. For the past three days, he lived in a world consisting of only his cell, the day and night, the windowsill's resident snail, and himself.

Alan parked up when he heard someone open the door. It was Lucas in his human form. He took one look at Alan and laughed so hard that he came close to dropping the goblet of water he carried.

"Sweet Mother of Belial, you look pitiful. I didn't think biting you would take such a toll on you."

Alan's excess—but weak—energy stored from the past days fired his sudden anger as he raised his head, growling. "You know why I'm like this. I have had neither a crumb of food nor a drop of water for the past three days."

"Well, did ya eat the meat I gave you?"

"No. I am now a monster by your bite, but I refuse to act like one."

Lucas rolled his eyes and grunted. "It's your fault that you never ate, not mine."

Alan eyed the goblet in the man's hand. Lucas noticed him watching and set it on the floor a few feet in front of him. Even though Alan knew he couldn't break free from the chains, he reached out for the cup as a baby would fumble for his mother.

Lucas watched Alan. "You want it?"

Alan ignored him and continued to stare at the goblet.

"I'll give it to you," Lucas said as Alan looked up at him eagerly. "For a price."

"What is the price? Will you kill me if—if I refuse?" The young man wheezed.

Lucas picked up the goblet and held it in front of Alan's face. Right as the elf tried to drink from it, the man pulled it away and put it by the boy's lips again—tantalization at its worst. "Vow your allegiance to Master Benedictus."

"Who?"

"Master Benedictus. He's the one who sent me to you the night I bit you."

"Never. I'll never betray my friends."

"Yeah, but Master Liam sure did. Your so-called 'friends' are worthless. They'll never accept you once they find out about your problem. They'd know by the dark hair you'll grow on yer chest that something's wrong."

"They will accept me no matter what the situation."

"Are you sure?"

Alan then remembered how disturbed Morwen was when she confessed to him about her nightmares. *Now that her horrible dreams—more like premonitions—have come true*, he muttered to himself, *wondering if she'll react to him the same way she did to the "him" in her nightmares.*

Alan hung his head. "I—I don't know."

Lucas set the goblet of water down in front of him and grinned. He turned in place and walked out of the cell, rumbling, "Make your decision before tomorrow night. I'll be listening for your cries for mercy."

Alan looked back to the goblet and then looked to the ground. He fought with himself about what decision to make.

"Wait," Alan said.

The stout man stopped in his tracks, listening intently.

"I'll join you. Please, just direct Liam and the girls away from here. That's all I ask."

Lucas smiled, ran to the goblet, and swiped it up with his huge, grubby hands. He held the cup to Alan's lips, and he drank greedily, heavily gulping down each drop.

"Your fate is sealed, boy. You're a servant of Master Benedictus now. And yes, I'll tell him of your request."

Lucas turned to walk away, but Alan asked, "Won't you unchain me?"

"We don't want you double-crossin' us, do we?"

Alan shook his head.

Howling with laughter, Lucas left the cell.

Later, around midnight, Alan jumped awake when Lucas swung open the cell door, letting it crash against the stone wall. He let the noise echo before his lips stretched into a smile across his chipped, yellow teeth. "Yer little girlie friend and her buddies are here."

"But I thought you said you *wouldn't* lead them here!"

"You're so stupid, boy. You trusted someone you just met."

Alan fought with his binding chains as Lucas roared with laughter.

"Don't worry; I'll make sure that the girls have a *very* nice stay."

"No! If you touch them, I'll—I'll—"

"Do what, *kill me?* With *those* chains and *these* thick stone walls, you're going nowhere, boy." Lucas left the cell, slamming the door behind him.

Alan was alone once again.

Chapter 16

Morwen could hardly keep herself from fainting with excitement. Her heart raced at the thought of finally getting the Brand removed. She gazed in awe at Kain's shiny, black, stone entrance hall, taking care to memorize every detailed painting and flickering torch. Lyn stood next to a stiff Liam and quietly fawned over him.

Liam somehow couldn't get into the happy spirit of their arrival, which struck Morwen as a bit strange. She didn't really pay much attention to it, though. She was too caught up in her own fantasy to really care.

Suddenly, a middle-aged man with long, silvery hair appeared at the top of the staircase. He wore a regal red robe with a short train that dragged behind him. His skin was a bit pale, but that was expected from someone who lived in such a cold, mountainous region.

The trio gazed up at this majestic man. Morwen wondered to herself who he was. He opened his arms warmly and bellowed, "*Welcome*, friends, to my castle!"

"Are you Kain, the wizard?" Morwen asked breathlessly.

The man's brow furrowed, and he replied, "Master Kain has gone on an errand to a far away town, but he will return in a few days. Please, you and your friends can stay here in the guest rooms while you wait for him. Do not worry; you will be safe with us."

"Who are you?" Lyn asked.

"My name is Nicholas Victor Benedictus. I am sure that you do not want to recite my entire name whenever you want my attention, so just call me *Master Nicholas*."

"Master Nicholas," Morwen asked. "Since your master won't be back anytime soon, could you please help us find our friend, a young man named Alan?"

"Who?"

"Alan. He has long, copper hair that's pulled into a braid. It's long enough to reach a little ways past his belt."

Nicholas paused in thought and folded his arms across his chest. "I have not seen anyone like that around here. Oh well, we *all* can look for him in the morning. It is getting late, and I am sure all of you need rest. Come, I shall show you to your rooms."

Morwen, Lyn, and Liam followed Nicholas up the staircase and through a maze of drafty, torch-lit passages. Nicholas first stopped at a pair of heavy wooden doors. The thousands of frightening goblin faces carved into them grimaced at their guests. Both Morwen and Lyn cringed at the sight and glanced at each other.

Nicholas seemed to notice, and he rested a reassuring hand on each of their heads. "Do not worry, young ladies. This room is less intimidating than you think, and it is very, very safe."

He swung open the door and ushered them in. The relatively small chamber housed a regal four-poster bed and a large, wooden closet. Unfortunately, the room held a faint—but rank—scent in its air. Lyn's nose wrinkled and Morwen's lips pursed tightly. Liam waved his hand in front of his face before Nicholas announced, "You, with the short brown hair, shall sleep here tonight. Please excuse the smell; this chamber has not been used for *quite* some time."

Lyn coughed. "I see." Keeping her eyes on Nicholas, she approached her bed, dropping her belongings onto its silky green covers. She gave Morwen a disappointed grin and said, "I'll be fine, Morwen. Go ahead and find your room. We all need our rest."

Morwen nodded and allowed Nicholas to lead her and Liam out of the room and into the cold hallways. They came to an enormous spiral staircase, which seemed to be tall enough to reach the moon. Nicholas, Morwen, and Liam climbed hundreds of steps until they finally reached the staircase's highest point. Morwen wondered why her room was so far away from Lyn's, but she held her tongue for the moment. *I'll ask when we arrive.*

Morwen glanced out of a nearby window, her head spinning when she saw that the trees below looked hardly larger than her fingernail.

The only room on that floor of that tower, a small bedroom, was where Morwen's would sleep. It looked—and smelled—much nicer than Lyn's room, and it consisted of a sturdy oak four-poster bed—silk, aqua sheets decorated it—and a small, ebony dresser with a mirror that reflected the setting sun. An enormous marble balcony with billowing gauze curtains finished off the breathtaking bedroom.

"It's . . . beautiful." Morwen sighed, her hand touching her lips as she studied her gorgeous chamber. Its walls, a pure white marble, contrasted the rest of the castle.

"This room has the best view in the entire castle—*besides Master Kain's*, of course."

"Why am I so far from Lyn? If you don't mind, I would much rather have a room closer to my friend."

Nicholas frowned. "Do you not like this place? It has all the finest furnishings in the land, but it is still not good enough for you?"

Guilt swept over Morwen. "No—No, of course not. This place is gorgeous. I really don't deserve it. I just wish it was closer to Lyn. I feel safer when I'm near my friends."

"Here at Kain's castle, we are all friends. Don't worry. We will all keep you from harm. And don't be so modest, please. I enjoy pleasing such a fine guest as you. This one of the more . . . special guest rooms."

Morwen nodded graciously. "Well thank you, then."

Nicholas bowed deeply and left the room with Liam. Morwen flung her bags onto her bed and rushed for the balcony. She gently pulled the delicate curtains out of her way and gazed out into the large, forested valley below. The feisty oranges and blazing reds of the setting sun danced on the swaying tree tops. Morwen rested her head on the white marble railing, wishing she could share the moment with Alan.

"Is he okay?" Morwen asked the sunset. "Please let him be alright."

She stayed in her place, daydreaming and remembering, until the moon floated up to its perch high in the heavens. Amazingly, the glowing, celestial rock was nearly a complete circle in the dark sky. *What a beautiful full moon there will be soon.*

Just as Morwen turned to enter her room, desperate screams and yelps echoed from the ground far below. She spun around, but someone grabbed her arm before she could peer over the edge of the balcony. Her Brand burned when she was touched. The pain alerted her of only one thing.

"An ene—"

Nicholas looked her straight in the eye and said soothingly, "Young lady, please do not look down. That is just a criminal we had to execute. He tried to break into the castle and hurt you and Lyn. There is nothing wrong; go to sleep. You need rest."

The Brand spread up her shoulder and onto the first half of her chest. Dizziness crept up on her as well. Morwen cringed but tried to hide her suffering as best as she could.

"Are you well?"

"Y—yes . . . I'm—I'm fine."

Morwen shook her forearm lightly to signal Nicholas to let go. He released her and watched her retreat to her bed. Breathing heavily, Morwen sat upon her right hand, which squirmed under her.

Nicholas, cocking his head, asked, "Are you *sure* that you are well?"

Morwen nodded quickly when she saw Nicholas advancing. He rested his thin hand on her shoulder, and her right arm writhed violently. Morwen breathed deeply and shut her eyes, trying to hide the fact that her arm was about to fly up and attack Nicholas. The scales crawled across her chest with needle-like pricks. It stopped suddenly.

When Morwen made eye contact with Nicholas, she relaxed and yawned. "I'm very, very tired. Please, just let me sleep."

"As you wish. If you need my assistance in anything, just open this locket. It will summon me at once." Nicholas placed a ruby-stoned necklace on her bedside table. He backed away with a deep bow and left the room.

Morwen sighed and rested her head on a fine feather pillow. Curious about the strange locket, she leaned over, plucking it from the table. Her fingertips tingled when they touched its golden chain. She held it in front of her face, and the tingling became small pinpricks.

Chills rolled down her back as she examined its detailed engravings. Famous demons and villains from folklore danced in a complicated ring around the gem. A certain figure in that circle caught her eye. Possessing featherlike long hair and a hooked nose, his picture was much larger than the others. He bore a familiar grin, and his harvest moon eyes made Morwen uneasy.

"Tobias." she said. "How could *he* be on this? This is Nicholas's locket."

Morwen turned the walnut-sized locket over in her hands and noticed a young man looking up at her with his hot pink stare. "*Liam?*"

She ran her fingers along the rest of the engravings, and the pinprick sensation changed to a slight burning. Startled, she dropped the necklace onto her collarbone. The gold's brilliance rusted into a greasy grey, and her Brand, now burning like hot oil, spilled across her skin. Morwen looked down at herself and watched the Brand's turquoise scales creep across her chest and a small distance up her neck.

Sweating frantically, Morwen tried to move the locket, but it stuck to her skin. She pulled as hard as she could to remove the cursed jewelry, but the chain scorched her hands. The Brand stopped moving up her neck and began to crawl down her torso.

Morwen thrashed about on her bed, rolling around and kicking to try and make it stop. She fell off the bed and continued to squirm. A handkerchief peeked out from under the bed, and Morwen desperately snatched it from its hiding place. She covered her hand with the cloth and grabbed the locket's chain. She lifted the necklace off of her chest and hurled it across the room. The locket smashed against the wall, its gem shattering easily. The Brand stopped.

Magenta smoke billowed from the broken jewel, and a long-haired man emerged from the cloud. "You called me, young lady?" Nicholas asked.

A bit flustered at her sprawled-out position on the floor, Morwen's mind searched for an answer. She became drowsy once again, and her throat and tongue grew dry. "I am quite thirsty," she said in a daze.

"Aren't we all."

"Excuse me?"

He cleared his throat and said, "Do not mind me. I—I am speaking to myself."

Nicholas produced a silver goblet with a wave of his hand. Its clear contents sparkled brilliantly.

Morwen sipped the water. "Thank you."

"Sleep well."

"Yes, you too."

Nicholas bowed, his silver hair brushing the floor, and faded into nothingness.

Morwen sighed and pulled herself onto the bed. She let her face melt into the valley of silk pillows and quickly fell into a deep, dead sleep.

Curious morning sunlight stung Morwen's sleepy eyes. The striking sunrise peeked over the tree-speckled valley below the castle. Glancing across the room, Morwen spotted the shattered ruby locket, lifeless on the stone floor. Morwen slid out of the bed and picked it up with the handkerchief.

"Strange." She clutched it in her covered hand. Morwen turned to walk out of the room, but she stopped when a pair of extremely handsome, blue-skinned men appeared at the door. Their strong, exotic bat wings distracted Morwen from her original task.

"Please, stay," they droned in unison. They opened the doors of the large oak wardrobe in the corner and revealed the two outfits lying inside. The outfit on the left consisted of a thin, rosy purple blouse with bell sleeves—accompanied by a dark brown bodice—and long, beaded leather pants.

The outfit on the right was much more elegant—an evening dress. Its ice blue fabric shone in the light, especially its thin, white silk sleeves and high neckline. Light blue shoes rested on top of them.

"Are these for me?"

"Yes. Choose the left one. Right one is for tonight."

"Tonight?"

"Master wishes that his guests attend dinner with him."

"Thank you."

"We are glad that we please you, Mistress." They bowed and left for the door.

"But I'm not your—"

The door to her bedroom slammed shut.

"Mistress."

A bit confused, Morwen changed into the new set of clothes—remembering at the last minute to put on her glove. She felt a bit odd wearing the bodice—she preferred a supportive corset—but she was still grateful for the new change of clothing. She thought it oddly convenient that the blouse had a high collar. More focused on meeting Lyn this morning, Morwen decided to think about her odd new clothes later on.

Morwen left her room in the tower to meet Lyn at the front doors of the castle.

Lyn, her face was blank with concern. "Morwen, I *need* to show you something."

"Me, too, but you go first."

"Alright then." Lyn led her friend to her room. "Well, last night, the strange smell in here got stronger, and I could have sworn I heard something rustling around in my room. I also heard—whatever it was—croaking like a hoarse frog."

"Did you see what it was?"

Lyn blushed. "Uh, no. I was so scared that I buried myself in my covers for the rest of the night."

She laughed. "*How courageous.* It seems like this wizard's castle is getting stranger by the moment."

"Why?"

"I heard noises last night, too."

"Really?" Lyn pushed open her door and led Morwen to her rotted wardrobe. "The smell seems to come from here, but the doors won't open."

"Are they locked?"

"No, and I even tried wedging them open with a knife. They refuse to move."

"I have no clue what's going on, Lyn. The noises *I* heard were coming from the dungeons. Master Nicholas said that they were killing a prisoner or something."

"Weird. So, what was it you wanted to show me?"

Morwen reached into her pocket, pulling out the broken locket wrapped in the cloth.

Lyn's eyes widened at the sight of the golden engravings. "Amazing! This pictures villains from children's stories. Look, there's Torrent, and Sanjo the Flatulent—Oooh, there's Tobias."

Morwen flinched.

Lyn examined all of the well-known fiends until she found the villain with the bright pink eyes. Her smile melted into a worried frown. She raised a thin, brown eyebrow, confused. "Is *this* . . .?"

"At least, I think it is."

"How could *Liam* be on here, Morwen? He wouldn't hurt anyone."

"*That's* what I saw as strange."

"*What* was it that you thought strange?" Liam asked, behind them.

Morwen jumped, and Lyn's hands flew to her mouth with the locket still dangling from her fingers. Liam's black hair fell over his face.

Lyn shook her head. "Nothing!"

"Then what is that in your hand?"

"A—A necklace Morwen has—no, uh, *got* last night."

"May I see it?"

Lyn looked to Morwen, who nodded warily. Lyn handed the broken locket over to Liam.

Liam held it in front of his face and examined each character in the gold. His eyes stopped at a particular picture, and his tan skin paled. He crammed the necklace into his pocket. "This is mine! Where *ever* did you find it?"

"What?" Lyn asked.

"This necklace is mine. I lost it last night. It has some of my favorite villains from fables, especially the one with the pink eyes," he said, rubbing the image with his thumb. "When I was very small, I used to scare my friends because I resembled him."

"But Master Nicholas gave that necklace to me last evening," Morwen added. "It can't be yours."

"Then Master Nicholas must have found it and given it to you in my absence. I went for a long walk last night in the garden."

"We were supposed to stay in our rooms. He didn't want us to wander around at all," Morwen countered.

Liam's nostrils flared, and he balled his hands into white-knuckled fists. With a swish of his black trenchcoat, he and his heavy brown boots stomped out of the room. The door crashed shut.

Utterly bewildered, Morwen and Lyn spent a few seconds in stunned silence.

"What was *that* all about?" Lyn asked.

"I think I have a clue, but I'll tell you after breakfast," Morwen said. "My stomach is practically eating itself. We have to meet somewhere private, though, so how about we talk in the rock garden behind the castle? I saw it out a window as I climbed down the staircase this morning."

"Alright."

Morwen and Lyn set off for the dining hall on the castle's second floor. When the two girls joined Master Nicholas and Liam for the meal, they acted like nothing happened, despite Liam's heated glares at Morwen.

He definitely wasn't acting like himself. After a short morning feast of eggs, bread, and cooked ham, Lyn and Morwen snuck out into the quiet rock garden.

The morning sunrays shone on the two girls as they weaved between structures of amethyst and agate. The sandy garden hissed as they walked, and moss and vines covered the white walls fencing in the area. The girls continued in silence until they found a large, pointed formation of blue agate. Morwen sat down behind it and pulled Lyn with her. Morwen looked around to ensure they were alone.

She leaned in closely to her friend and muttered, "I don't think Liam is what he seems to be."

"What?"

"He's hiding something from us. He isn't acting like he usually does."

Lyn nodded in agreement, a little hesitant. "Yes, and I miss his old self. I was stunned when he took that necklace away. Do you think that Liam is an enemy? I surely hope he isn't."

"Of course he may be an enemy! The snatching of the locket, the glares during breakfast. Something is definitely wrong."

"Well, should we tell Master Nicholas?"

"Definitely, but he said that he'll be busy today, but whenever we see him again, we'll reveal Liam's secret."

A gust of wind whistled through the rock garden. Lyn was in the process of coming to her feet, but she swayed, feeling faint, and sat back down. Morwen became dizzy, and her vision blurred. She forgot what she had just told Lyn. The breeze died, and Lyn said, "Isn't it such a beautiful day today? I'd like to go look around the castle grounds more. Would you like to come with me? I wanted Liam to join me, but I don't know where he is."

"Of course. Let's go."

Morwen, feeling well again, came to her feet. The two friends talked loudly while they weaved in and out of hedge mazes, fountain clusters, rock gardens, and statues. Before they knew it, the sky faded from bright blue to orange and red, and the golden sun started slipping under the horizon. Morwen and Lyn went their separate ways, hurrying to their rooms to prepare for dinner.

Chapter 17

Morwen gazed at her face in the mirror. A blanket of dirt darkened her cheekbones, and her nose and eye sockets shone with a light sweat. Grimacing, she thought, *I cannot go to dinner like this.* She turned to the washbasin and water pitcher on the dresser. After setting the pitcher's cloth cover aside, she wrapped her clawed fingers around the pitcher's handle carefully, slowly.

The porcelain crackled when she applied even a hint of pressure from her palm. Morwen lifted the pitcher with her other hand and poured the clear, cool liquid into its accompanying bowl. She bent over, flipping her hair out of her face, and cupped her hands. She splashed cold water onto her face. Her claws nicked her when they brushed her lower jaw.

Morwen's normal hand flew to her dripping chin. Her fingers floated across her skin until they met a small slit below her lip. The cut stung at the touch, and a little blood dripped onto her thumb. She stepped in front of the mirror to watch the scrape mend itself.

"Good," she muttered, moving back to the basin. She plucked the pitcher's cloth cover from the table, wiped her face dry, and tossed it next to the basin. Her hands barely squeezed the rim of the basin when she picked it up, but her Branded hand still chipped the fine porcelain.

Sighing in exasperation, Morwen lifted the basin with her safe hand and left the room to toss the dirty water off the balcony. After returning the bowl to the dresser, she opened her wardrobe to take out her fine evening dress. Having learned her lesson, Morwen—rather awkwardly—dressed herself with her one safe hand.

The young woodland elf frowned at having to wear a gown, but she did admit its icy blue tone was quite beautiful. She especially liked that it covered her scales. Although she knew her secret was safe with Kain and his subordinates, she still felt very uncomfortable showing the Brand to strangers. Stepping into the fine, tall-heeled shoes, she tottered over to the mirror again.

Though the dress's high neckline and unnaturally long sleeves concealed the Brand's scales, the dress did not hide Morwen's messy hair. She searched the room for a brush.

"Aha," Morwen said, opening the top dresser drawer. She sat on the bed and pulled the brush through her long green locks, occasionally glancing at herself in the mirror. At last, she stood and examined her finished self. Her hair *did* look better, but Morwen deemed it too informal for a dinner with a wizard's apprentice.

Now, how do I plait hair again?

She tapped her fingers on her mouth few moments, thinking. Morwen sat back down on her bed and spent the next half hour accenting her hair with thin plaits, occasionally poking herself in the head or eye a with her claws. Once she finished, she did not need to glance at herself again; she already *felt* stunning with her extravagant hair and dress.

Morwen strode to the balcony, gazing at the early setting sun. She breathed in the fresh mountain air and thought, *If only Alan could see me like this.* She shook her long, green locks and turned her back on the warm scene. Often tripping in her delicate shoes, she descended the tower steps to meet Master Nicholas for dinner.

Two handsome men—much like the ones who had shown her the new clothing—welcomed Morwen at the dining hall doors. They swung open the heavy doors to the hall. Lined with torches, the dining hall glowed with warmth. An immensely long cherry wood table stretched down the middle of the chamber, and tall-backed chairs bordered the masterpiece. Master Nicholas was already sitting at the head of the table on the far side of the room. Liam sat to his right.

Nicholas wore a rich indigo robe with a large, ruffled collar. Numerous golden rings shone on his fingers. Liam, on the other hand, donned black boots and a simple, snowy white servant's robe. His jet black locks had been pulled into a neat ponytail.

Glad that she had dressed herself well for the occasion, Morwen drifted over to Nicholas. The fine-mannered man stood up from his seat and kneeled before her. His metallic grey hair spilled onto his buckled shoes.

When Morwen approached him, he took her hand and placed a soft kiss on it. She blushed half from discomfort and half from flattery. Nicholas stood up and pulled the chair to his left from its place. Morwen lowered herself into it, and he slowly pushed it in.

Morwen glanced at Liam, who smiled warmly at her as if the incident that morning had never taken place. Extremely sharp teeth peeked out from his grin. Sitting up straighter in her chair, Morwen swallowed hard. Her eyes darted from Liam to Nicholas and back again.

"Um, Master Nicholas?"

"Yes, milady?"

Milady? Morwen thought. *Strange.*

Looking back at Liam, she froze. His smile grew larger and less friendly the longer she stared at him. On the brink of panic, Morwen broke eye contact and asked, "Where's Lyn?"

Liam's grin grew a bit larger. "I saw her walking around outside only minutes ago. I have the feeling she might have gotten lost."

Morwen stood up. "We should look for her, then."

Nicholas shook his head. "No, we shall start without her. I am sure that she will arrive soon."

Morwen sat back down and glanced at her pewter plate and silverware.

Nicholas clapped his hands, and the two winged men appeared. Each carried a large platter in his hands. One man carried a metal tray with three wine glasses perched upon it. Two held a thick, dark red liquid, but the third glass contained only crystalline water. The other man's tray held only a cooked salmon that steamed lightly. Nicholas and Liam took the two glasses of red liquid.

Morwen received the salmon and the goblet of water. She picked at the delicious fish with her fork, trying to eat to be polite. A nervous sensation pulling at her gut ruined her appetite.

"Does the salmon appeal to you?" Nicholas asked after he sipped his drink.

Morwen hastily stuck a piece of the fish into her mouth. After chewing and swallowing, she piped, "Yes, it's delicious!"

Liam smirked and took a loud gulp from his glass. He placed the cup back onto the table with a loud thud. He leaned forward, resting his head on his hand, and asked, "Morwen, how do you like the castle?"

"I like the rock garden very much. It's very peaceful in the morning,"

"The garden will be yours, soon."

"Excuse me?"

Nicholas threw Liam murderous look. His smile dying, Liam sat back in his chair. "Never mind."

The dinner went on in an awkward silence, and Lyn never arrived. Morwen eventually finished her food and stood up. Sudden dizziness shook her. "If you'll please excuse me, Master Nicholas, I'd like to go look for Lyn."

"You may go, but will you please come with us to your balcony, first? We would like to show you something that I think you will like."

"Um, alright, then. Lead the way."

Nicholas smiled. "Excellent. Thank you."

They hurried to the end of the dining hall and slipped out the door. As Nicholas, Liam, and Morwen trekked up the seemingly endless flights of stairs, she tried to piece together all the strange happenings that day. Suddenly, it came to her. *He's a vampire.*

Now, worried about Nicholas's wellbeing around Liam, Morwen's stomach tightened. The three of them finally made it to the doors of her room. Liam pushed the doors open, and Nicholas walked to the edge of the balcony. The last tongues of sunlight illuminated his face. Liam, still in his white robe and black boots, joined him at his side.

Morwen approached them, and once she also was beside Nicholas, he put his arm around her, causing an uncomfortable chill to roll down her back

She tried to hide her discomfort. "Master Nicholas, before you show me anything, I need to tell you something," she said as she eyed Liam.

"What is it, my dear?" *Dear?* The term was more than unsettling.

"It's Liam. I think he's a vampire!"

Nicholas's eyebrows rose as he faced Morwen and pulled her closer to him. This made Morwen more on-edge than before. He chuckled, then burst into hysterics. Throwing his head back, he laughed to the heavens. Like Liam, razor-sharp canine teeth emerged from his mouth. His blue eyes flickered a poisonous yellow.

"My dear, my apprentice is not the *only* one here who thirsts for blood."

Morwen gasped and squirmed in Nicholas's cold grasp. His great strength kept her still.

"Do not worry, my sweet. I do not think that Tobias will mind if I make you mine, also."

"Tobias?" Morwen asked, struggling to escape. Her heartbeat quickened.

"Lord Tobias is as much your master as he is mine. I have been ordered to stop you from reaching the wizard Kain's castle."

"What are you talking about? T—Tobias isn't my master."

"Do not play dumb, my sweet," Nicholas cooed as he stroked her face. "You know very well that your infinite service to him is near."

He seized her right hand and pulled off the glove. He tossed the covering off the balcony and clutched Morwen's clawed hand. Her bones crackled and quivered in his tight grip. His evil touch forced the Brand to continue eating her skin.

Morwen cried out, her voice darting aimlessly through the valley below.

"You are his chosen, young elf. And you are *my* chosen as well!"

Morwen tried to shove Nicholas away as his jaw lowered. The strength in her scaled arm was not enough to slow him. His fangs grew even longer and more menacing as Morwen fought to pry her arm from his grip.

The sun fell behind the mountains, suddenly shrouding Morwen and the vampires in candle-lit gloom. The full moon inched into the sky. The master vampire's fangs lowered to Morwen's neck. She cried out for help over Liam's laughter.

Morwen used all her might to try escaping Nicholas's control, but the pain from the spreading Brand weakened her. Giving up at last, she shut her eyes slowly, awaiting a telltale pinch on her throat.

Just as Nicholas's breath brushed her skin, the bedroom door crashed open, and the vampire looked up. A large wolf, its fur the color of mahogany, stomped on two feet through the doorway.

"*Liam*," Nicholas hissed. "Why is that creature still alive?"

"Neither Lucas nor—nor *I* thought he would break free, my master."

The wolf roared and pounced on Liam. The pink-eyed subordinate vanished from the scene in a thick cloud of bats. Now that its original target was gone, the wolf turned to Nicholas.

Nicholas shoved Morwen to the floor and trembled, backing up to the very edge of the balcony. "Stay back, beast!"

Morwen, stricken with terror, could not bring herself to move.

The wolf stomped up to them and snorted in Nicholas's white face.

Nicholas clawed and hissed.

The werewolf's hand-like paw flew to the vampire's throat and held him over the railing like a beaten doll. With a snort, the beast flung Nicholas off the tower and howled to the stars.

Morwen, finally controlling her fear, scrambled to her feet and backed away. She did not dare to look down and see the face of the screaming vampire plummeting to the ground.

The squeals for help bounced off the sides of the valley, then stopped suddenly. A little confused, Morwen hurried to the ledge and met a thick flock of ravens that flapped past her face. The wolf struck out at the birds. High-pitched laughter echoed through the valley and faded away.

Morwen turned to gaze, terrified, at the wolf. It watched her for a second, but then bent over and roared at her. Its thick saliva flew everywhere in stringy globs. Morwen backed up as the seven-foot-tall wolf approached her.

Out of instinct, she raised her clawed hand to defend herself. She prepared to swipe at her attacker, but some odd feeling in her gut held her back.

Morwen shook her head and tried to get into her warrior mindset, but her will still barred her from doing anything. Realizing that her arm had failed her, she dashed for a nearby sword hanging from the wall.

She unsheathed it and held it in front of her, ready to call upon Armando's training to defeat the monster. But when the wolf charged at her, she decided that all she could do was run.

Kicking her shoes off, she darted out of the room with her sword in hand and stumbled down the tower steps. The wolf rumbled down after her and gained on her every second. Morwen finally found the end of the stairs and leaped off its end. Swinging around every corner in the maze of hallways, she heard statues crash to the floor and paintings shred behind her as the wolf pursued her.

She reached Lyn's room and pounded on the doors. "Open up! Please!"

The heavy doors opened to a bedroom packed tightly with the walking undead. *That explains the smell*, Morwen thought.

She noticed a wide-open wardrobe in one corner. *Had Lyn disappeared through some kind of portal?*

"Lyn?" Morwen called as she cleaved through each living corpse. Nobody answered. A bony hand grabbed her shoulder, and she turned around quickly. A broken body, its short brown hair all dirty and ragged, swayed on its feet before her. This creature's skin wasn't as rotted as all the others, but its flesh still showed deep bites and scratches.

Morwen's stomach churned. "Lyn!" she shrieked. A million thoughts rushed through her head after shoving her friend away.

Lyn fell over and twitched on the floor.

Is this real, or just a spell? Should I save Lyn, or should I come for her later? What should I do? Morwen cried out in grief. She looked up from Lyn to find the wolf approaching her from the doorway.

Morwen glanced at her friend. "I'll come for you later!" Striking aside the undead that swarmed her, Morwen burst out the door, running right past the werewolf.

Morwen made her way to the entrance hall of the black castle. She stumbled, falling onto the floor's rough stones. As she sat up, the wolf thundered towards her. It slowed its pace, falling onto all fours, and stopped right over her. It breathed in her face.

"Could you possibly make this situation any worse?" She shouted before looking to the monster's face. The wolf paused and sniffed her curiously, then whimpered. Morwen gazed into the creature's eyes and found the poor soul trapped inside.

"Alan?" Morwen asked quietly, remembering her dream. The wolf whined, and his tail fell between his legs. Morwen brought herself to her feet and warily held out her hand. Alan growled threateningly, and she recoiled so suddenly that she lost her balance and fell to the ground.

He shook his head and stopped. Careful not to move to quickly, Morwen stood once more and put her hand in his large, humanoid paw.

"Alan." Morwen hugged his furry torso. He growled again, and the young elf prepared to jump away from him and draw her sword. Once again, he breathed heavily, calming down. Alan picked up Morwen ever so gently and cradled her in his arms. Although he was docile at the time, Morwen's stomach tightened at the thought of him mauling her or hurling her into a wall.

Doing her best to stay on high alert, she shook her head as exhaustion crept up on her every moment. Alan took her out of the castle and into the chilly, crisp night air. Morwen's eyes drooped shut. She breathed out, dropping her sword, and fell asleep, listening to the warm thump of Alan's heartbeat.

Morwen awakened next to Alan in the middle of the woods. His tattered pant legs gave him a drowned sailor's appearance, but his river of copper hair revived his noble look. Alan's bare chest rose and fell in a pained sleep. It was early morning, and the sun had just started peeking through the trees. Morwen, not wanting to remember last night, shied away from him and walked to the trickling creek nearby. Sitting down on its damp bank, she watched the water rush by. Tiny tadpoles struggled against its current.

Morwen heard Alan sigh awake. She glanced around for only a moment to see him rubbing his muscles. Crossing her arms, she stared back at the water.

Alan came up to her and sat at her side. "Good morning."

Morwen didn't even blink.

"I'm sorry about what happened to Lyn—and me."

Morwen slapped the water, scaring the tadpoles into the reeds. "Sorry? For what? This is completely *my* fault, Alan," she snapped, glaring at him. "I was careless back in the castle. I should have taken action when I could have, but my memory... I kept on forgetting my plans whenever I made them."

"You might have been under a spell, you know."

"A spell? Maybe, but how do I excuse abandoning my friend? I could have saved Lyn if I wasn't so busy with trying to save myself. My best friend is a walking corpse because of me." She hung her head.

"She isn't that way because of you. Nicholas lured you into a trap, and—"

"I fell right into it. What was I doing? I was anything *but* heroic."

"We can try to go back and save her, you know."

Morwen calmed down, realizing that she'd overlooked an obvious idea. She twirled a claw in the water and asked, "Yes, but what can we do about you?"

"I'll be fine."

"No, because I know that it hurts when you change," she said, holding up a finger to keep him from responding. "But we have much more important things to do than argue. We need to go back and save Lyn, but I don't know where we are."

"*I* know where we are."

"How?"

"It's odd, but I just—know."

"I don't think we should act on instinct right now."

"Yes, we can. Remember the elven teaching that a Peach fish always knows where its birthplace is? Somehow, I know where *I* was 'born.' Nicholas's castle is just over the two hills over there," he said, pointing to the rise in trees to their right.

Morwen sat up a little taller and realized that Alan's guess was all they had. She stood up. "Lead the way, then."

Alan came to his feet also. "Certainly."

The two of them stomped up one hill and the next until they found the eerie structure's gates below. They held hands for stability as they ran down the steep slope to the castle. Alan's balance failed when he slid on a loose ledge of dirt and tumbled down the hill. He let go of Morwen's hand and rolled to the bottom.

Morwen finally caught up to him and laughed a little. "Are you alright?"

Dusting himself off, Alan came to his feet. "I couldn't feel better," he said, smiling at her.

"Then let's get going."

Morwen, her heart swelling with excitement, crept up to the front gates and slipped inside. She hurried to the massive front doors and grabbed a thick iron handle. With her great strength, she pulled the door open to reveal the flame-lined, obsidian front hall. Without even thinking about Alan behind her, she burst through the large chamber and up the staircase towards Lyn's room.

Once she came to the last few steps, the entire castle shuddered and shook. Pillars cracked . . . the floor shifted and jumped. Dust and pebbles melted from the ceiling like rain, and picture frames dissolved into sand on the floor.

Morwen ran even faster up the stairs. She leaped onto the top step to find a gaping hole in its place. She fell through, hitting the ground below, and the entire castle fell into a massive pile of ashes on top of her.

Silence. Morwen tried calling to Alan but ended up inhaling a lungful of the dark dust. She coughed and wheezed as she brushed the mess away.

The overcast sky finally appeared above Morwen, and she breathed out to rid her lungs of the last bits of dust. The valley did not tremble in fear of the castle anymore. No crows squawked to trespassers, and no more streams quivered in the fortress's shadow. For once in a very long while, Morwen experienced utter silence and solitude. *Have I gone deaf?* She asked herself, her ears ringing.

Alan's calls answered the question for her. "Morwen? Morwen, are you alright?" Alan asked, running over to help her from the musty tomb.

"Of course I am. But what about Lyn?"

"We should start digging for her."

Both elves had just started the search for their friend when a cold sensation overcame them, and a strong gust of wind flung the ashes into their faces. Their skin, eyes, and noses burned from the ruined castle's remains soaring around them and up into the sky. When the breeze calmed, fresh fall air filled their lungs. Morwen and Alan rubbed their eyes open.

Morwen frowned. "Why were you laughing just then? This was not funny at all. The castle is gone, and so is Lyn!"

"I wasn't laughing."

"Then why did I hear someone laugh a moment ago?" Morwen asked. She thought for a moment, and her eyes widened. "We have to leave."

"Why?"

"Something is here with us, and I may have an idea of who it is," she said, turning around and sprinting into the woods.

Alan followed and shouted, "But don't you want to search for Lyn anyway? She might be nearby."

Morwen shook her head. "I don't know where she could have gone, but she is *not* here."

Alan caught up to her and said, "First you wanted to look for Lyn, and now you abandon her. I don't understand."

Morwen ran faster. A tree fell behind them. "Someone *wants* us to stay and look for Lyn, and Nicholas is that someone! His leader will use all his power to distract us from getting to Kain."

"Leader?"

A tree snapped in half next to them. Morwen glanced behind her and saw two pure white figures following them. Her heart skipped a few beats. *What are those things? Maybe they're not Nicholas and Liam.* Her breath grew heavier, and her limbs ached and weakened. She *had* to outrun whatever was pursuing them. Her pace slowed, and Alan passed her, then looked over his shoulder.

"Do you need help?" he asked.

Morwen, wincing, shook her head and sprinted ahead of Alan. In moments, she fell to her knees.

"Are you sure you don't need help?"

"No, I'm—fine."

Alan stopped and scooped her up into his arms, continuing their flight through the trees. He smiled for a moment and laughed.

"What?" Morwen asked.

"This reminds me of a similar event many months ago."

Morwen grinned tiredly. "But this time I don't have an arrow stuck in my head."

"Yes, thankfully."

As Alan charged through the thickets, Morwen held her head near Alan's chest to prevent a sideways collision with a tree. Alan's chest expanded and sank faster with each moment. He eventually came to a stop, letting Morwen stand on her own.

He bent over and put his hand on his knees for support. "I haven't heard the strange laughing for a while. I think we're safe."

Morwen nodded. "Good, but now we need to figure out where we are."

She turned to a tree near her and dug her clawed fingers into the bark.

Alan frowned. "Don't get upset. I know we'll be able to find the real Kain's castle."

"I'm not mad. I'm going to see where we are."

Morwen wrapped her other arm around the tree trunk and pulled herself onto a branch. She worked her claws out of the wood and reached to a higher spot on the tree. She climbed to another branch, and then another until she reached the swaying top of the pine tree. The slight mountain breeze licked her face while she took in her surroundings.

The mountains surrounded the area, and the overcast sky brought a damp chill to the air. Morwen turned only slightly, and her foot slipped off her perch. She gasped and sank her claws into the tree trunk to catch herself.

"Are you alright?" Alan called from the ground.

"I almost fell."

"Please, be careful!"

Morwen hugged the trunk for stability when she craned her neck to look around again. She gasped again.

"Did you slip again?" Alan asked.

Morwen's arm stretched to point to the east. "No, I see it. I see Kain's castle!"

A strong, chilly wind blew in her face once more.

Chapter 18

Morwen and Alan reached a break in the thick mountain woods. The ground rose upward to a white marble castle that stretched to the sky. The palace's spires touched the passing clouds; its windows and walls, decorated in hanging moss, exuded a timeless elegance. Flocks of doves rested on the castle's black, wooden roof and cooed faintly. Morwen and Alan smiled at each other, knowing that their journey was at an end.

Morwen gawked at the glorious sight. She hugged Alan and cried, "We're finally here! We made it, Alan—together!"

Alan returned the embrace.

"And once we are finished here, we can look for Lyn," Morwen said softly. She pulled away from the hug and hurried to the castle doors.

Alan caught up with her and pounded on the thick, heavy oak gates. Nobody answered. He knocked again.

"Is Kain even here?" Morwen wondered. "The castle looks untouched, judging by all this moss."

Alan struck the door again. A muffled voice called from behind the thick wood. The door eased open, revealing a thin, hunched-over old man. *Is this Kain?*

His gentle, seafoam-green eyes glistened in contrast to his rich, brown skin. His fluffy white beard was twirled into a thousand tiny braids, and the mountain breeze billowed his lavender robes. His large ears twitched along with his bushy black eyebrows as he waved thoughtfully to his guests.

"Welcome, young people. I am Kain, the Master of Magic," he said, chuckling and rubbing his bare scalp. "And the King of Bald Heads. Now, who are *you two*?"

"Morwen. I'm pleased to meet you."

"Alan. It's an honor to meet such a legend as you."

Kain waved his hand, shaking his head, and said, "Thank you, but please, be as relaxed as you want with me. Bah, townsfolk these days. They treat me like a god, but I'm just a grumpy old wizard who just wants someone to chat with. Do you want to come in?"

"Yes, please," Morwen and Alan said in unison. They followed the elderly wizard inside.

Kain, with the help of his gnarled staff, limped through the castle's entrance hall and up numerous flights of stairs. "So, before you tell me about your problems, how about I get you two something to eat. Have you had breakfast, yet?"

"No, sir," Morwen said. She smiled when Alan's stomach rumbled next to her.

"Well, then. Follow me, and we'll have some cake and tea."

Dark, intricate tapestries and busts and pots and portraits overwhelmed the entrance hall. Morwen rubbed her eyes from the burn of dust in the air. The dim lighting that surrounded them made all the walls appear much thicker and closer. Morwen coughed a few times.

She leaned over to Alan. "This place is beautiful, but it is just so, so *old*."

Kain looked over his thin shoulder. "*Eh?* Did you say something, young lady?"

"Nothing, sir."

"Okay. Well, if you're complaining about the steep steps, I apologize. We'll be in my eating chamber in no time."

Kain led Alan and Morwen through halls of dull suits of armor, faded paintings, and cobweb curtains. Every once and a while, a bat would flutter from its roost and flee into another area. Morwen looked behind herself and saw their footprints in the filth on the scratched, wooden floor.

The thick air irritated her eyes and prickled at her throat, but she did her best not to cough too much. Morwen heart sank a little when they passed numerous vacant bedchambers and meeting rooms, echoes of the castle's past glory.

Apparently, no one lived in this gigantic castle except for Kain and the vermin nesting here. Morwen hung her head at the thought of this old wizard spending the last of his days in a dirty, old castle. As Kain said, his only visitors were people who pestered him with pointless questions and wishes. Morwen jumped out of her thoughts when Kain clapped his hands.

"Oh, here we are! The dining room—at least, one of the smaller ones. Come in and get seated."

Morwen and Alan made their way to the table covered in spider webs and rat droppings. Morwen lowered herself into a creaky mahogany chair, and when Alan sat down next to her, his chair snapped in half.

Kain turned around after closing the door. "I'm so sorry! Here. I'll fix this place up." With a twirl of his wrinkled fingers, the wizard did away with the grime on the table and replaced it with an elaborate display of little cakes and cups of tea. Alan's chair flipped onto its feet and mended itself with a loud *zzzzzzip!*

The young elf brought himself to his feet and sat on his repaired chair. The old man rested on a throne-like, ebony seat. His eyes widened excitedly when he snatched a few light blue pastries and a small cup of peppermint tea. Morwen and Alan watched him happily eat.

He stopped a moment, staring at them. He said through a mouth of cake, "Help yourselves; I can always conjure up more."

Morwen slowly plucked a pink, squishy cake from the display and bit into it. Its sweet, berry taste brought a small smile onto her face. She hesitated, then grabbed all the pink pastries she could find. She placed them all in a pile on a nearby plate. Alan chose a cup of peppermint tea from the collection of drinks.

"So where are you two from?" Kain asked.

Without thinking twice, Morwen knew she could trust this kind, old wizard. "I'm from Aren, and Alan here lives in a cottage between Aren and Terra's Hollow."

"Terra's Hollow, eh? Did you two have to pass that cursed field to get here?"

"Yes."

"Incredible. You must be a brave pair!"

"Thank you," Morwen chimed after she swallowed another cake. "We've come to ask you if you could—"

"Make you more cake? I'd be delighted," Kain interrupted.

Morwen looked at Alan. *I guess I can delay removing my Brand for a while. A few hours won't hurt.*

Those hours soon turned into a day of stories, laughter, and good food in the evening.

Kain offered Morwen and Alan a place to stay for the night. "Are you two married?" he asked as they strolled through the dark halls.

Both elves glanced at each other and blushed.

"No," Alan said quickly. "Not *quite.*"

"Then I'll give you separate rooms. Here, young lady, you can stay in here."

Kain directed Morwen into a small chamber of lavender bed sheets, white marble walls, and ebony furniture. "I'm sorry I can't supply you with new clothes. Yours look pretty beaten up right now."

"Oh, no. I'm perfectly fine. Thank you, still."

Morwen's large, dark windows flashed white, and a faint rumble shook the glass.

Kain chuckled and said, "Looks like there's a storm comin'. Nevertheless, sleep well. If you need anything, Alan and I will be in our rooms down the hall."

Morwen thanked him again, and Kain shuffled out of the chamber. Alan gave her a warm smile as he shut the door. The bedside candles flickered before another flash illuminated her room. The loud hiss of rain beat on the castle.

Lifting the musty covers off the straw mattress, Morwen lay down on her dust-ridden bed. She tucked herself in, pulling the covers up to her ears, and let her mind wander. She slept.

An earsplitting crash shook Morwen awake. Her heart shivered behind her ribs. The candles nearby had extinguished themselves long before Morwen had awakened, but the constant flashing of lightning allowed her to see, if only briefly. The bellow of thunder shook her bed, and Morwen could swear she heard someone trying to talk amidst the noise. The rain pounded upon her windows, creating strange, oozing shapes as lightning lit them from behind. Morwen glanced at one window, and the light nearly blinded her. She screamed and yanked the covers over her head. Her heart pounded in her throat. The outline of a twisted, fleshy Grog from Sanguine had appeared in her window. Although her room was hundreds of feet off the ground, Morwen still trembled under her covers. Before she could calm herself, something struck the door to her room. She shrieked again and coughed from the dust laced in her blankets.

"Go away! Leave me alone!"

Her room door flew open, and rushed thuds came up to her bed. It was too late. Strong hands gripped her covers and tore them from her grasp. She squirmed and kicked to try and escape. A warm hand grabbed her face. Now, Morwen knew this was the end. *But wait*, Morwen thought. *Grogs have* cold *hands, not warm.*

Another flash of lightning made the room flicker. Alan stood above her. "Morwen, are you alright?"

"I'm fine. I just . . . got a little scared."

"A *little*?"

"Fine. I was terrified. You can go back to your room now. I'll be fine."

"No. Something's happening to Kain. He's shouting and calling for help from down the hall. I need you to help me break his doors down. They're apparently locked from the inside."

Morwen jumped out of bed and ran barefoot with Alan down the hallway. They came to a pair of heavy wooden doors. Alan pulled at the lock, but the doors still wouldn't open.

Morwen paused and wondered, "Do I pick the lock with my claws?"

"No. Just break it. We have no time to spare!"

Morwen raised her black talons above her head and swung then down onto the doors' lock. The rusty metal shattered in an instant, and Alan kicked the door open.

"Kain, are you alright?" Alan panted.

The old wizard dropped a floorboard back into its place and stomped it roughly to secure it. He smiled and said, "Of course!"

"Then what did you just put in the floor?"

"Oh, just a few potions to ease my sleep. I was yelling because I had a terrible nightmare! Don't fret, Morwen and Alan, go back to bed."

A grin crept across his face until he was smiling from ear to ear. Morwen and Alan sighed in relief, and they both bid him good-night. The two elves shut the door and walked back to their rooms.

Morwen frowned. "Poor Kain. He's lonely, he lives in a dirty castle, *and* he has nightmares every night."

"It seems like he has everything under control, though."

"But it's upsetting knowing he'll die all alone."

"I'm glad that you care so much about others, Morwen, but right now, you need to worry about yourself."

"Why?"

"It smelled . . . *strange* in his room."

"That's probably old man stench, Alan."

"No—I mean—lately, I can smell things better than I could before."

"Since when?"

"Since I got bitten," Alan said.

Morwen stared at the ground.

"That room smelled of blood," Alan said gravely.

"Kain *can't* be a vampire, too."

Alan placed a hand over her mouth as Kain's door creaked open, and the wizard peeked out and looked around. Alan nudged at Morwen to walk faster, and he whispered, "Just get back to your room. Something isn't right. I can feel it."

"And this happens *just* when things seem to turn for the better."

"*Go*. I'll join you later so I can protect you."

Morwen darted down the hall in her dirty evening gown. She made her way to her room and climbed into her bed again. She could not relax, though. Her mind swirled with the possibilities of what might be going on. By the time Alan entered her room, Morwen had fallen asleep from sheer exhaustion. Her dreams reminded her that she hadn't spoken to Kain yet about the Brand. Her dream-self decided to ask him in the morning.

The sunshine spilling through Morwen's windows created colorful rainbows on the floor. She could have cared less, though, about the pretty scene. She sat up, excited and alert as ever; her nerves prickled when a gentle knock came from the door.

"Morwen?" someone called.

"Yes?"

"It's Kain," the voice hummed. "Alan is right here, too. He said you have something to ask me. Come to my study."

"Wonderful," Morwen said. She leaped out of bed and followed Kain. They climbed hopelessly steep staircases for a very long while. Morwen whispered to Alan about how she thought it strange Kain could walk up the steps so easily.

"Who knows?" Alan muttered. "He's a wizard. You don't know what kind of magic could be helping him."

"Last night unnerved me a little, that's all. I'm just being cautious."

"We had a bit of a scare last night," he said. "But everything will be alright now."

Kain led them down a long corridor to his private study and showed them to two large armchairs. Morwen sank into the soft—but very dusty and worn—chair and sighed. Alan rested in the seat next to her.

Kain conjured up a padded stool and a cup of hot herbal tea for himself. The wizard happily sipped his drink. "So what do you want from an old troll like me, Morwen? I have all the answers over there in my desk."

Alan cocked his head. "You're a troll? I thought you were a wizard."

Kain threw his head back and laughed before looking back at him. "Ah, no. It's a mere jest. I'm human. If I was a troll, I'd be too old to try to carry a club around, anyway."

Morwen thought a moment before she said anything. The message on the back of her bedroom door flooded into her mind like fresh blood: *Tell anyone about it, and you'll take responsibility for your family's murder.* She hesitated for a few moments. *I hope I can trust him. I guess I don't have a choice, though.*

Morwen sighed and looked the wizard right in the eye. "I have this . . . curse on me. It's called a *Brand*. The Dark Wizard Tobias placed it on me in plans to kill King Dragomir. I've been told that you're the only person who can remove it."

Kain reached out his hand and said calmly, "You've been told right. Please, come closer. Let me see that Brand of yours."

Morwen hopped up from her chair and stood in front of the wizard. He grabbed her clawed hand. Morwen gasped, wincing from an unexpected jolt from the Brand. Alan leaned forward in his seat, curious of what was going on. Suddenly, Kain's skin bubbled and melted from his flesh. Morwen tried hitting him to loosen his grip, but he was too strong. The last of his skin oozed off him, and the absence of his wrinkly pelt revealed a daunting man with pale, yellowed skin and bright crimson hair. Morwen crumbled to her knees, succumbing to the pain of the Brand. The new man cackled.

Morwen's eyes widened. "How—How did you get here, Tobias?"

"I'm pleased that you actually fought off Nicholas, Morwen. I felt I just *had* to come and congratulate you on your victory, but the old coot was the only person standing in my way. Don't worry; I *took care of him* with ease last night."

"You're sick," Alan growled. He flew to his feet, but before he could step forward, Tobias flicked a finger and bound his feet to the floor.

"Morwen," Tobias hummed. "Is *this* your little knight in matted fur?"

Tobias squeezed Morwen's hand tighter, and she cried out, falling motionless.

Alan glared at Tobias and snarled, "Let her go."

"I'm afraid I can't do that. But I *can* help you find a place in Mister Garouf's colony."

"Did *you* plan my bite?"

Tobias clapped, purring. "Excellent use of logic, Mister Saratogas. I have no prize for your efforts, but I give you most sincere condolences for taking Morwen away."

Tobias picked up Morwen and carried her over his shoulder. Alan fought with the spell on his feet. Tobias cackled and faded into nothingness, taking Morwen with him.

"Good luck finding us, mutt," said his disembodied voice .

The instant the villain disappeared, the spell on Alan broke. He stomped on the floor and swore under his breath, glaring at every object in the room and cursing each one. He paused when his eyes came upon a desk overflowing with paper—parchment, pictures, notes, and more.

Alan rushed to the study area. He sat down on the rotted wooden stool by the desk and began to shuffle through the pillars of stacked spells and scrolls. One group of notes, in particular, caught his attention. His heart leaping in his chest, he picked the paper up and read it carefully. The smile on his lips grew with each line he read.

"Outstanding . . . "

Chapter 19

Morwen awakened on a warm stone block, her vision slightly blurred after she opened her eyes. She glanced around and found herself. Her eyes finally corrected themselves, and she gasped at what she saw in detail. She rested on an island of rock, surrounded by a lake of steaming, bubbling magma.

I'm in the heart of Sanguine.

Suddenly, the shrieks of the condemned shot into Morwen's ears, but the din—thankfully—was not as loud as it used to be.

Morwen tried to sit up, but thick restraints held her to the stone.

Tobias appeared in a puff of smoke. "Celebrate! This is the greatest day of your life yet."

Morwen scowled at him. "My willpower will keep me strong. I won't submit to you!"

Tobias's hair—along with his eye sockets and scars—darkened to a rich red shade, and his skin paled. His eyes grew large in excitement, and he grinned from ear to ear. "Oooh, it seems like you've picked up a bit of a mouth on your trip." Mimicking the first time they met, Tobias paced around her in a circle, watching her carefully.

He pouted a little. "I'm disappointed. The Brand didn't spread as much as I wanted it to. That's alright, though. A little help from me will do the trick. "He reached out to her with a bony hand, set his palm on her forehead, and pressed against her skull.

Morwen bit her lip, holding back a cry as an invisible lightning bolt ripped through her. She thrashed and clenched her fists. Her muscles flexed against her skin. Her veins bulged, her body tingling and stinging from the pain. Morwen watched

Tobias's smug expression, and she used all her energy to keep from screaming.

"I'll never give in," she said weakly. Sweat shone on her face. Tobias made a crooked smile and dug his black nails into her scalp. Morwen winced as the Brand swooped across her skin and swallowed it whole.

Black, antelope-like horns sprouted from her forehead. A long, lizard-like tail tipped with spikes extended from her spine. Now, both of her hands bore claws, and small fangs peeked out from behind her lips. When Morwen's new body relaxed and fell limp on the stone, Tobias peeled his hand off her head and took a few steps back. He studied his work with a few nods.

Morwen, exhausted, still did not give up her fight. "No matter how I look, I will never be your servant."

"I'll only release you from that rock if you pledge your loyalty to me—not that you have a *choice*, really. I just want the enjoyment of hearing it from your pretty little mouth."

"Forget about it, then."

The Dark Wizard held his hand over her, and an unseen force tugged at her lips. She tried to fight it, but the power was much too strong. It wrenched her mouth open and strummed her vocal chords. "I shall obey."

"*Forget about it, then!*" Tobias mocked with a snicker. "I just made you say it. Oh, I have the feeling that this is going to be lots of fun!"

Morwen scowled at him while he unbuckled her restraints. She hopped off the slab, flexing her clawed fingers, and—as a new sensation—twisted her tail. She did her best to straighten out her muddy, sweat-stained dress when she fully came to her feet.

I might as well look nice if I am going to stay like this.

"Come," he said, turning around. He walked down the granite pathway that led from the island.

Morwen waited for a few moments before she whipped her tail at Tobias from behind. Without turning around, he held his hand out to his side, and Morwen's tail wrapped itself around her neck. As it slowly constricted her, its spikes pulled across her throat. The pointed tips stretched her scaled skin open until small streams of blood trickled down her neck. Tobias flew around and grabbed Morwen by the chin.

His eyes bulged when he smiled. "If you don't want your conscious mind *completely* erased, you'd better not try anything nasty anymore." He giggled with a wag of his finger, then commanded her tail to release her. Her bleeding wounds mended themselves.

Nodding in defeat, Morwen followed her master to his lab.

Days passed, and the future grew more hopeless for Morwen as every hour slinked by. Tobias gave her a single black robe and a pair of leather shoes, since her dirty evening gown was most unsuitable for a dark wizard's apprentice. The only thing keeping the Brand from swallowing her soul was her strong willpower to remain—mostly—in control. Tobias pressed constant lessons and challenges on her to try and break her resolve.

Several weeks after Morwen's transformation, a scrawny, two-legged creature stumbled past the laboratory door—an Underling, the lowliest of beings in Sanguine. Morwen sat dolefully on a stool in a corner of the room, thinking the three-foot-tall creature quite bizarre with its peach-colored skin, visible spinal cord, and stumpy, forked tail.

Then Tobias's hair bleached itself white, and her hair stood on end. While Tobias continued to stare at the Underling, he threw his hand to the side, beckoning Morwen to approach him.

"Come," he said in a monotone.

Morwen realized his plans. "No, I won't."

"I said *come*, girl." He made a fist. Invisible strings wrenched her off the stool, and she approached her master despite her resistance. The Underling passed the doorway again, and Tobias's hand became a flat palm that swooped over Morwen's head, pointing towards the creature. An unseen rope tied itself to her and tugged her across the room, forcing her to sprint out the door. Tobias clapped once inside his lab, and Morwen snatched up the creature by the neck.

The Underling stared at her with its huge, orb-like black eyes, and its pointed ears fell flat on its skull. The quivering being cried like a wounded mouse in Morwen's hand. Tobias met them outside, and he grinned maliciously.

He bent over and whispered into the Morwen's ear, "You can come out, now."

Morwen's vision blurred, and she heard her own voice say, "Hello, do you remember me?"

"Yes, and I prefer you to go back where you belong."

The Brand controlled her speech once again. "Please, we're almost one person! Let us be friends rather than enemies, and it will make things a lot easier for *both* of us."

"Never."

"*Ladies*," Tobias scolded jokingly. "How about we focus on the task at hand, *hmmm?*"

The world became a blur to the real Morwen. She relied on her other four senses to figure out what actually was going on. She sighed deeply and focused.

She heard Tobias's hand swing past her ear, and the Underling left her hand. Her arm swiped the air, and it hit a lightweight, bony object. After a desperate squeal rang through the tunnel, a warm, red liquid splashed onto Morwen.

"That was lots of fun, was it not?" the Brand asked cheerfully.

Morwen's rage and grief broke the Brand's command over her. Her vision returned to normal, but she shut her eyes tightly to avoid seeing what she had done. She ran into Tobias's lab.

A similar event happened every day from then on, which led Morwen to wake up every morning with a feeling of agony for both herself and her next victim. Each time she was forced to fight, Tobias pulled and pushed on Morwen with invisible strings, commanding her every move and heartbeat. Guilt overcame Morwen whenever she took another life. After finishing each deed, she always ended up sitting in the corner of the lab, hugging her knees and sobbing as Tobias returned to work. Tobias always whined over his shoulder that tears were a sign of weakness, but she never listened to him. Morwen had a conscience; he didn't.

Though she never took notice of it, Morwen's powers amplified and became more potent each time the Brand controlled her. Her tail's spikes grew sharper and eventually seeped a deadly toxin. Her claws hardened enough to where she could climb up walls, and her skin became stronger than the finest chain mail.

Although she tried not to give up hope of escape or rescue, Morwen soon realized her dreams of freedom were almost hopeless. She'd left Alan at Mt. Schism, halfway across the continent, and even if he made it back home safely, she wondered if he even had a chance at finding Tobias's lair.

Numerous times Morwen wanted to just give in to the Brand, but a tiny voice inside her kept pushing her to wait just a few days more.

One afternoon—or night, Morwen couldn't tell from being underground—Tobias was experimenting at his workbench with various herbs and animal bones.

Morwen, nearly bored out of her mind, entertained herself by kicking a pebble around the room. She suddenly missed the rock at one point and accidentally stepped on it. Her strength crushed the stone into dust. She sighed, sulking, as she walked towards the doorway of Tobias's lab.

Without looking up from his work, Tobias said, "Morwen, come here."

"Why?"

"Do not question my authority. Come."

The elf shuffled up to her master. She gazed at the odd potion he'd been creating. Tobias handed her a fern leaf from his pile of herbs. "Drop this into the bowl."

Morwen let the fern fall in, and the potion liquid turned a sick yellow. The wooden mixing bowl melted with a hiss, and the yellow substance oozed off the workbench. It wiggled on the floor, then slinked out the door like a fat slug.

"Incredible," Morwen said.

Tobias rested a hand on her shoulder. Morwen began to smile at his gesture, but she froze. She found it a bit strange that he acted so kind towards her.

Tobias looked down his bent nose and grinned. "Congratulations, Morwen. You just sent a deadly plague into the world."

Morwen's eyes welled with tears, and her scaly hands covered her mouth in shock. Her grief melted into disgust. "You're a sick person, even by demon standards."

"I take that as a compliment," her master said with a bow.

The girl could hardly stand at the wave of emotions tossing her conscience about. Morwen dashed out of the room, fleeing to her sleeping quarters and throwing herself onto her bed. She sobbed into the rough bed sheets. "Why did I fall for that?"

Morwen hit her wall in anger, and a large crack opened from the impact. She pulled away from the wall and held her hand in front of her face. Her reflection glistened in her vicious, black talons. Smooth, turquoise scales had replaced her once flawless skin. Morwen was not the beautiful angel she used to be. She was now a demon, a fiend: A *fallen* angel.

"What is happening to me?"

"*Me*," the Brand responded.

"No! Go away."

"I can't leave. I already have a foothold on your entire body. Well, all of it except for that elusive soul of yours."

"*Sure* you have. Except I'm strong enough now to stay in control," Morwen scoffed. She regretted her bluff when her tail started wrapping around her neck. Slowly—oh so slowly—it constricted her.

The Brand made her smirk. "See, Morwen? I have *much* power over us." The tail squeezed even tighter. Morwen's skull throbbed from the blood trapped in her head, and she wheezed shallowly.

"I even have the power to *kill* us," She said, almost breathless. Her tail retreated from her throat. "But I won't, since that would only infuriate Master Tobias."

"Leave me alone!"

Morwen's cry rang throughout the chamber, and when the Brand did not respond, she knew she had won the battle—for now.

As more time passed, Morwen started to forget about Alan. Her time became greatly occupied with keeping the Brand off her soul and ensuring she didn't anger Tobias too much.

Then, Morwen woke up one morning and found out that Tobias planned for her to kill Dragomir in two days' time. "You can't be serious!"

Tobias leaned against her room's doorway. "I am, actually."

Morwen's heart sank. No one could save her now. She slumped out of bed in her wrinkled black robe. She mentally prepared herself for the terrible crime she would soon commit.

Tobias headed off to begin working, so she followed him to spend another day of killing feeble little demons.

Since there was nothing else decent to do, Morwen used one of her claws to scratch pictures into the wall. Amidst the tapestry of random squiggles and animal pictures, she made one crude sketch of a young boy and girl holding hands.

They smiled warmly at each other. She stopped and stared at it for a few moments, then drew pointed ears on each figure.

A strange, warm feeling lit her heart like one of Lyn's matches. The corners of Morwen's mouth stretched into a hopeful smile on her fanged jaws. She scooted closer to the picture and carved a wedding veil on one elf, and a knight's helm on the other. Morwen suddenly noticed that she had drawn the hats on the wrong characters, so the veil shrouded the boy's face, and the girl wore armor.

First giggling at the mistake, Morwen soon burst into full laughter.

Tobias, a bit concerned by his quiet apprentice creating such a racket, asked over his shoulder, "What are you doing?"

Morwen swiped at the picture to destroy the carving. Her claws screeched on the wall as rocks crumbled to the floor. Morwen avoided eye contact. "It's nothing."

"If you're destroying my notes over there, I'll skin you alive."

"But I'd heal in a heartbeat," Morwen said, a bit of defiance in her voice.

Tobias turned on his heel and glared at Morwen. A thin finger jabbed at her in the air.

His nostrils flared. "Tomorrow. *Tomorrow*, I am going to make your Brand devour that wretched soul of yours!"

Morwen gasped. This was not what she had planned. Alan appeared in her mind for the first time in a long while. He smiled at her, his mouth slowly falling into a straight line. Morwen imagined his brow furrowing at the thought of her leaving him forever. Before she could worry any more, a hooded figure appeared at the door of Tobias's lab.

The stranger wore a necklace that held a black, ruby-encrusted key.

Morwen's eyes widened. *King Belial: in his shorter, more human form.* Once he made himself known by clearing his throat, Tobias glanced at him and dropped what he was doing. He kneeled before his master. Morwen followed suit.

"Tobias," Belial rumbled.

"Yes, Master?"

"I have gotten word that you are planning to take revenge on King Dragomir soon. Is that true?"

"Y—Yes, milord. I deem my weapon, Morwen here, ready for the challenge."

Belial crossed his arms and shook his head. "My rival wields more power now than he ever has before. The girl needs a greater form of protection than the Brand on her skin."

"Then what do you propose I do?"

The Branding

"Let me cast a spell on her for even greater strength. I need to take her into the official chamber to perform the ritual."

Tobias looked up from his bent knee. "May I accompany you?"

"You may not!" he roared, shaking the ground. "You know that my ritual rooms are off-limits to all."

"Y—Yes, Master. I trust your judgment," Tobias said, scuffling a few inches backward.

"Good. Now let me have the girl."

Morwen stood up and approached the king of Sanguine. Her knees trembled, and she hoped she would not fall and make a fool of herself.

Belial waved his hand in dismissal to Tobias, and he led her out of the room. He walked with her up the steps, and Morwen asked cautiously, "Excuse me, King Belial, aren't your quarters in the other direction?"

Belial spun around and pointed a gray, bony finger at her. "Do not question me, child!"

He turned back to the front and stomped up the stairs. Following him once more, Morwen shut her mouth. They eventually came to the top of the steps, which stopped at an opening to a lush pine forest. They emerged from Sanguine and stood in the fresh woodland air.

"Why are we out here?"

"I'm saving you from that twisted imp."

"But you're the king of Sanguine!"

"No," he bellowed as his cloak bubbled and melted away from him. A regal, yet poorly-dressed young elf stood before her. "I am just a *very* lonely 'knight in matted fur.'"

Morwen gasped. "Alan! How did you . . . ?"

"I beat Tobias at his own game. I found a spell or two in Kain's study and used them on myself. They were identical to the ones Tobias used on *us*. I found Tobias's place of residence, too, and I hopped on a horse I found near Kain's paddock behind the castle. The stallion and I spent these past weeks riding here."

Morwen threw herself onto Alan and hugged him tightly. He paused for a few moments to stare at her tail and horns, to gawk at her scaly skin and clawed hands. He sighed and hugged her back.

Morwen could not contain herself. "Oh, thank you for saving me! I—I don't know what I can do to repay you. I—Wait, what's wrong?"

Alan released her and shook his head. "I apologize for taking so long to arrive. Look at what he's done to you...."

"It's not *your* fault." A little overwhelmed to be out in the open, Morwen glanced around her. The doorway to Sanguine sat inside a large boulder. Morwen's eyes widened, and she cried, "Alan, this is near Aren! Oh please, may I go see my house? I just want to have a glance at it after so long."

Alan's soft brown eyes looked to the ground, then back up to her, and his face grew pale. "You don't want to see your home now."

"Why, what happened?"

"I heard that if you told someone about the Brand...."

Morwen dashed towards town, leaving Alan trailing behind her. She did not care if she was running into town looking the way she did; she *wanted* elves to be there. She wanted to deny the thought that kept drifting to the front of her mind.

Morwen came to a charred clearing.

Thin strings of smoke billowed from the remains. Morwen's small, once lively town rested as a pile of black ashes before her. She could feel the air grow colder around her as her eyes studied the scene in silence.

Unable to grasp that her childhood home was gone, she wandered through the streets, stumbling left and right. Only a charred wooden frame remained of the inn; a street over, a bakery-turned cottage lay peacefully on the ground, its fresh loaves of bread changed into smoky bricks; Master Armando's cabin was a pile of splinters and pebbles; Morwen's haven had fallen victim to hell.

She fell to her knees at what was left of her house. Digging through her home's wreckage, she called, "Mother, Mother! Brynn! Brynn, come out!"

Alan snuck up behind Morwen and swung his arms around her. He brought her into a rough hug and dragged her from the burned ruins. She kicked and thrashed wildly, her face sticky with soot and tears.

She sobbed and muttered, "It's entirely my fault. All those innocent lives are gone . . . because of me."

Alan kneeled down next to her and placed a warm hand on her shoulder. He tried his best to calm her. "Don't blame yourself, Morwen. Tobias tricked you into telling. *He* is the one who did this, not you."

Morwen sniffed and wiped the black tears from her cheek, ignoring him.

"Come to my hut, Morwen. We can stay there for a while to hide from Tobias. There, we can decide what to do next."

"All right."

Back in Sanguine, Tobias was growing impatient. He sat at his lab table, prodding a cockroach with his finger. "What is taking him so long?" He mumbled. Another few minutes passed, and he grew more impatient. Tobias stood and left his lab to find the ritual chamber. He passed the throne room on the way there, and he spotted Belial on his giant black seat. "Ah, he must be finished," Tobias said.

He approached King Belial and bowed. "Master, are you finished with the girl?"

"What *girl?*"

"My weapon to destroy King Dragomir."

"*I* do not have her."

"But, milord, you said you would place a protective spell on her."

Belial cocked his head and scratched it. "I *did?*"

"Yes, only a half an hour ago. Did the spell backfire and erase your memory?"

The Dark King pondered for a moment. Suddenly, Belial balled his hands into fists, and he roared in his subordinate's face. "DAMN IT, TOBIAS, YOU'VE BEEN TRICKED!"

Tobias nearly tore out his own hair. His mind flew to a certain copper-haired elf he had left at Kain's castle. Tobias's hair burst into white and almost stood on end. His eyes flashed bright red, and he twitched from barely-restrained fury.

His mouth twitched as he giggled under his breath. "Alan, you sneaky, dirty little pup, I'll make sure that your pained howls won't *always* be to the full moon!"

Chapter 20

Alan carried the grief-stricken Morwen to his hut. He let her rest on his bed and pulled up a chair so he could sit nearby.

Morwen sat up, her eyes narrowing to hide tears. "My family is dead. That's all that concerns me now. I know how awful I look like this, but I can't find the energy to care anymore. I'm destined to look like this from now on. With Kain dead, no one can take the Brand off me now. So be it."

Alan cupped her chin in his hands. He looked right into her eyes. "I think you're beautiful, no matter how you may look at the moment. You still accept *me*, even though I change every full moon. Don't get too discouraged; you won't be this way for long."

"What do you mean?"

Alan smiled. "A spell for my disguise wasn't the *only* thing I found in Kain's research." He pulled a wrinkled piece of parchment from his pocket, then held it up for her to see. "From what I read on this note, the only way to get rid of a Brand—if no spells are able to—is 'to kill the master to whom the curse's host is Branded.'"

"But beings like Tobias are immortal. *Nothing* can hurt them."

"Let me finish. The bottom of this paper explains that the only way to kill a demon—like Tobias—is to create a *Mortis*."

"A Mortis?"

"It says here that it's a special kind of arrow that shoots through an evil immortal's chest to kill it. It looks like the Mortis is made up of three parts. The Mortis's long, wooden body is to be carved from the wood of a Ciarran ash tree. Its feathered tail is to be soaked in blood drawn from a vampire, and its tip must be the fang of a werewolf—and that tooth won't be coming from *my* mouth, mind you. I don't want you to risk the chance of getting bitten by me."

"I can handle myself very well, thank you," Morwen said, smiling slightly. "But all those other things worry me. How in the world will we collect them if we don't know where they are?"

"I guess we'll have to start looking as soon as possible."

"Definitely."

"But enough of this. I'm hungry. I'll make us some dinner." "Good. I'm starving"

The day melted into evening, and evening fell to night. Morwen sat cross-legged in front of a row of four stones by a tree. The smooth rocks displayed the painted phrases: "For Gwendolyn," "For Mother," "I'm sorry Brynn," and "Thank you, Armando."

Morwen's heart became sank in her chest as she read each time she read the epitaphs. She denied over and over again that all four of them were gone—forever. *Maybe they weren't at home when all this happened. Maybe they escaped. Maybe they went into hiding somewhere.*

"I miss you all already." Morwen glanced at her scaly palm, and the aching inside her bubbled into grieving rage. She came to her feet and struck the tree's rough trunk, tears streaming down her cheeks.

"Lyn... Mother... Brynn... Armando... *Why?* Why did this happen to you?"

She struck the tree again, then again. "You three can't be gone; it's impossible... You can't leave me."

Morwen's knuckles throbbed as she hit the bark.

She paused when a leap of delusional logic came to her. "If I let the Brand control me, I'll gain enough power to kill Tobias. Yes—yes, I think that plan just might work. I don't need a Mortis; I need sheer power." She shut her eyes and breathed in deeply...

Alan came out of the hut for some fresh air and saw Morwen near the four memorial stones. "MORWEN, STOP!"

He ran up to her and hugged her tightly. "Please, whatever you were doing, don't do it. You can't let this thing in you win. You survived for a month in Sanguine by sheer willpower, so you can survive a little longer now. I can help you, Morwen, and you can help me. We can get through our hardships together."

Morwen opened her eyes and hugged him back. "Yes, together."

"You know, I'm wondering also if Lyn's out there, with your family and Armando, too. Maybe they're being kept somewhere safe until it's time."

"Time for what?"

"I don't know yet, but my instincts are telling me that they might not be dead after all."

Morwen smiled, small tears blurring her vision. "I hope your instincts are right."

"Then don't give in and disappoint them if they *are* still alive."

"I'll hold on as long as I can."

"Come. Sit with me in the tree. I'm sure there's a beautiful view from there. It'll help take your mind off of all this for a while."

Morwen and Alan scaled the tree together. They sat on a branch near its top and talked for a while—not about their quest, but about everything else: childhood memories, jokes, stories. They watched the moon rise in the sky, and they watched it in silence, enjoying each other's presence.

Alan gently took Morwen's hand in his. Morwen, grinning, rested her head on his shoulder—she made sure not to hit him with her horns. They both gazed at the glowing crescent perched atop the forest. The woods hummed under them. The cool night breeze muffled the owls' lone hoots, strengthened the bitter smell of sap, and brightened the fireflies' golden flashes of light.

Morwen sat up straight and looked at Alan and his strong, handsome features. He turned to her and grinned. "What?"

Morwen smiled, bit her lip, and asked slowly, "May I—May I kiss you?"

"Why do you have to ask?"

Morwen sighed. "I don't know if *you'd* want to—"

Alan leaned over and pressed his lips against hers. Morwen's world spun, flip-flopped, and turned upside down as Alan's warm breath spilled over her face. When they pulled away, and Alan murmured, "I'll always want to kiss you, no matter what you look like."

Morwen gazed into his eyes and realized, *I'm in love.* "Alan?"

"Yes?"

"I don't know how to say this, but . . . . "

Alan chuckled quietly. "I already know, but it would be nice if you could say it aloud."

Morwen never realized that it was so hard to just say, "I love you."

Alan held Morwen close. "I love you, too, and we'll get through this journey together, you understand? We'll do this *together.*"

"And together, we shall eliminate Tobias from this world . . . forever."

A raven leaped from its perch nearby and soared off into the night.

To be continued . . .

Allie Emerson Is Descended From
a Fairy Grandmother
She's Supposed to Save The World From Evil
But First She Has To Survive High School

More Great Fantasy For Teen Readers!

MOON SPUN
Marilee Brothers

Faeries, come take me out of this dull world,
For I would ride with you upon the wind,
Run on the top of the disheveled tide,
And dance upon the mountains like a flame.

...William Butler Yeats

    I am the Star Seeker, aka She Who Is Destined To Save The World From Evil Trimarks, bearer of the prophecy star in my palm, owner of the magical moonstone pendant, survivor of numerous Trimark attacks. And I just found out I'm part-fairy. People in the know spell it *faerie*.

    So I was nervous as I followed Ryker into the faery kingdom he called Boundless. The ground beneath us began to shake, and a voice that sounded like living thunder boomed, "You dare to bring this mortal into our world?"

    I clapped my hands over my ears, frantically looking around for the source of the fearsome noise. *Oh, this can't be good, Allie.* I made a move toward Ryker. Strangely, he was grinning like crazy and pointed to the pool and waterfall. "Over there."

I took a cautious step forward. All at once, something burst from the water, reared back and let loose with an ear-splitting bellow so frightening, I screamed in terror. The ground shook harder. Or maybe it was my legs. I froze in my tracks, even though my brain said, "Run, Allie, Run!"

The creature looked like a humongous black horse with moss-covered green scales growing out of its back, flaring nostrils and water weeds tangled in its flowing mane. Its mouth was open, exposing large, slime- green teeth.

"What . . . is . . . that . . . thing?" I gasped.

"Allie, meet Uncle Davey. Uncle Davey, this is Allie, " Ryker said calmly, as if I'd been invited for Sunday dinner to meet and greet the family.

"He's your uncle?" I squeaked. "He looks like a horse. Is he a horse?" The high-pitched sound grew louder, so painful I covered my ears again.

"Ari! Maddie! Stop laughing!" Ryker ordered. "She can't help it. She's a mortal."

I had no idea who he was talking to. I had other things on my mind, like staying alive. I weighed my choices: 1. Stuck in Boundless forever. 2. Eaten by a horse-like creature with big, green teeth. No contest.

I fished the nail out of my pocket and was about to toss it over my shoulder when the thing roared, "No! You will bury it twelve crunkles deep. Hawk, you will help her. Then, and only then, will I allow her to live."

I kneeled down and began scrabbling at the loamy soil. "How big are crunkles?" I whispered to Ryker.

"Don't worry. I know when to stop digging." He picked up a stick. "Stand aside. I'll do it."

I held my ground. "It's my fault. I'll dig the hole."

Ryker said, "Do not argue and do not get near me until the iron is buried."

"He said, stand aside!" Uncle Davey roared. Startled, I stumbled backward, tripped over my feet and plopped down on my butt. The high-pitched sound increased a couple of decibels. I prayed my head wouldn't explode. I scrambled to my feet. "Who or what is making that sound?"

Ryker kept digging. "The hedgerow pixies find you extremely amusing."

"Pixies?"

"Over there." He pointed at the hideous horse thing. "Sitting on Uncle Davey's head."

I took a cautious step toward the pool. Just then, Uncle Davey sneezed loudly and water shot out of his gigantic nostrils. The creature's violent sneeze caused two tiny figures to shoot straight up in the air where they hovered for a few seconds before fluttering down to land on his head again. They were shrieking with laughter, as if Uncle Davey was their very own bouncy castle.

Fascinated, I took another step. Ryker, who had apparently reached the magic number of crunkles, stopped digging. "I wouldn't get to close if I were you. Uncle Davey's still pretty pissed off." Ryker backed away from the hole. "Now, drop the nail in and cover it with dirt."

I buried the nail quickly. "What happens if it touches you?"

Ryker looked grim. "You don't want to know."

The pixies, who I'd mistaken for dragonflies, pushed off of Uncle Davey's head and zipped over to Ryker, landing on his shoulder. Thank God, they'd stopped laughing. I couldn't keep from smiling when I saw them up close. The bigger one was about four inches tall. Her straight, black hair was tied back with a tiny, glowing daisy chain and a tiara sat crookedly on the crown of her head. She wore a pink tutu and bell-shaped skirt that looked like—and probably was—made of rose petals.

She launched herself off Ryker's shoulder and hovered about six inches from my nose. My eyes crossed when I tried to focus, which caused another round of shrill laughter.

"I'm Maddie." She twirled around to make her rose petal skirt flair out. "I'm a princess. Can you tell?" Before I could answer, the other pixie flew over to join her. "No, sister. Not you. Me."

Maddie said, "This is my sister, Ari. She thinks she's a princess too." She flitted to my ear and whispered, "But really, she's not. I am."

Ari was shorter and obviously younger than Maddie. Where Maddie was tall and slender—at least for a pixie—Ari was sturdy. Dressed in pink cotton panties and a purple cape, her dark brown hair cascaded down her back in a tangle of ringlets. She scowled at her sister and thumped her chest. "I heard that. Ari is too a princess."

Maddie landed on my right shoulder and folded her wings next to her body. With a little shrug, she said, "Okay, whatever." She sounded so much like Nicole Bradford, I laughed out loud.

The two pixies were so cute, I couldn't stop smiling, at least until Maddie said, "It was Ari who did it, not me."

"Huh? Did what?"

Both pixies giggled hysterically. I put my fingers in my ears until they stopped.

Ari said, "We made wind blow under your dress during the parade. Ari saw your bare bum. Did you see it, Ryker?"

Ryker winked at me and grinned. "Oh yeah, I sure did."

My cheeks grew so hot, I'm surprised I didn't spontaneously combust. "Well, that wasn't very nice. How would you like it if that happened to you?"

By way of answering, Ari, still hovering in the air, flipped around, pulled down her little pink panties and mooned me. My jaw dropped in surprise. Really, I had no words.

"HAR! HAR!" Uncle Davey apparently thought Ari was hilarious. I'd had about enough of Uncle Davey. I was about to give him a piece of my mind, when he blew water at me and sank slowly beneath the surface. Now that the threat of iron was gone, Ryker stepped up close and rested his hands on my shoulders. Ari and Maddie touched down on the top of his head. "Pixies like to do mischief. They were just having fun."

"Wasn't so fun for me." I grumbled.

Ryker's eyes rolled upward. "Perhaps you two should apologize."

"Sorry, Avalon," the two squeaked in unison, then giggled and flew to the pool, landing on the only visible part of Uncle Davey, his flaring nostrils.

Alarmed, I called, "Be careful! You're really, really close to that thing's mouth."

Ryker chuckled. "Don't worry. Uncle Davey likes the pixies. It is humans that kelpies don't care for except, perhaps, for a snack."

"That's what he is . . . a kelpie?"

Ryker nodded. "They're also called water horses. You might want to keep your distance."

I shuddered. "Don't worry."

"Okay, then. You've met Uncle Davey and the pixies. We got rid of the iron. There's only one thing left to do before we move onward. Are you ready to meet your grandmother?"

Author Biography

Hey, guys! I'm Micaela Wendell, author of *The Branding*. I loved creating stories ever since I was very young, and I enjoyed reading just as much. I wrote my first actual story in late kindergarten, when I made a short story about the robins building a nest outside my bedroom window. When I was in grade school, I would almost always need extra paper for our many story projects. I'd just want to write more…and more…. and more… I never wanted to stop! Finally, around middle school, I decided to start writing a fantasy book. After two false starts in middle school, I began writing *The Branding* in seventh grade. Once I finished the very rough manuscript before my eighth grade year, my teacher Mrs. Schuster (author of *Flowers for Elvis*) acted as my mentor and assisted me in polishing the piece. She ultimately helped me get *The Branding* published, and it's still hard to express how thankful I am for her help. Getting published may look like an easy and speedy process, but don't get me wrong—this entire journey was *tons* of work, but it all paid off in the end.

Getting published was my dream, and I gave it my all to achieve it. You can reach your own dreams, too, if you're willing to put in the work. Find your talents, hone your skills, and go for it!

If you want to contact me, feel free to e-mail me at thebranding@hotmail.com. I'd love to talk to you!